'I've noticed caring for o Didn't you wa of your own you were married, Jacky?'

Jacky concentrated on spooning coffee into the cafetière so she wouldn't have to look at Pierre. 'I did have a baby…for a short time…but he died…' She swallowed hard.

He rose up and moved swiftly to put his arms around her. 'I'm sorry,' he said. 'I had no idea that…'

As she looked up into his eyes, Pierre could feel the trembling of her lovely, delicately formed, curvaceous frame as he held her close to him. He could tell that she was putting her trust in him, just as she had done all those years ago. But this time there was real, sensual emotion flowing between them. His initial reaction had been to comfort her, but now his feelings were of a different kind.

Dear Reader

The idea for my **French Hospital** duo came to me one hot summer day when I was picnicking with my ever-romantic husband among the sand dunes bordering one of my favourite French beaches. Not far from fashionable Le Touquet, and so quiet and tranquil, I decided that St Martin sur mer was the perfect setting for my two linked stories. That's not its real name, but perhaps if you visit the region and find yourself in a quaint little town with a hint of romance everywhere you explore, you may have found it.

This duo is about two medical colleagues, Debbie and Jacky, both doctors, who become friends while working together at the Hôpital de la Plage. Romance blossoms for both of them amidst the energy of the Accident and Emergency Department.

A VERY SPECIAL BABY was Debbie's story.

In A FAMILY WORTH WAITING FOR Jacky finds herself working alongside the charismatic Pierre Mellanger, her romantic idol from the past. Pierre broke Jacky's heart when she was younger because her love for him was unrequited. Dare she risk Pierre's rejection again?

I hope you enjoy reading these two books as much as I have enjoyed writing them.

Margaret Barker

A FAMILY WORTH WAITING FOR

BY
MARGARET BARKER

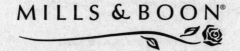

MILLS & BOON®

*All the characters in this book have no existence outside the imagination
of the author, and have no relation whatsoever to anyone bearing the
same name or names. They are not even distantly inspired by any
individual known or unknown to the author, and all the incidents are
pure invention.*

*First published in Great Britain 2005
Harlequin Mills & Boon Limited,
Eton House, 18-24 Paradise Road, Richmond, Surrey TW9 1SR*

© Margaret Bårker 2005

ISBN 0 263 84324 6

*Set in Times Roman 10½ on 12 pt.
03-0805-49695*

*Printed and bound in Spain
by Litografia Rosés, S.A., Barcelona*

CHAPTER ONE

JACKY could feel the blood draining from her face as she watched the newly appointed consultant of the Urgences department at the Hôpital de la plage coming in through the door of Marcel's office. The unexpected shock of seeing Pierre again after all these years was almost too much to believe so early in her working day.

It had been a big enough surprise when Marcel had called her into his office to explain that he was handing over his medical and surgical responsibilities in Urgences today. She hadn't had time to ask him any questions before the new consultant had arrived. But the fact that it was Pierre...so many memories, too many conflicting emotions...

The room seemed to be spinning around her. She felt dizzy. Everything was so unreal...

'Great to see you again, Pierre,' Marcel was saying in French, greeting his new colleague with a calm, welcoming smile and an outstretched hand.

Jacky reached for the nearest chair and sat down as she watched the two men shaking hands. Her legs felt as if they would buckle beneath her. Why on earth hadn't Marcel mentioned that he was leaving the department today? And, more importantly, why hadn't he told her who was going to replace him?

'Let me introduce you to Dr Jacky Manson,' Marcel said. 'Jacky, this is Dr Pierre Mellanger.' He turned back to the newcomer. 'Jacky worked with my wife, Debbie,

for a month, then replaced her when she took maternity
leave and…'

'Pierre and I have met before,' Jacky said shakily, ris-
ing a little unsteadily to her feet.

The colour had flooded back into her cheeks rather
more than she would have liked as she made eye contact
with the new consultant. She stretched out her hand towards Pierre, hating herself for longing to feel the touch
of his fingers against hers and desperate to appear calm
and unmoved by the encounter. This was the way she'd
coped all those years ago, when she'd known that her idol
would never dream of reciprocating her affection for him.

A bemused smile had appeared on Pierre's handsome
face and his dark eyes held a hint of enquiry as he took
hold of Jacky's hand to shake it in a brief, formal manner.

'Remind me, Dr Manson, when did we meet before?'
he asked politely, as he released her hand.

Jacky swallowed hard. 'Back in Normandy my mother
always insisted I was called Jacqueline. You weren't allowed to shorten my name when—'

'Jacqueline! C'est toi? Vraiment? Mais comme vous
avez changé!'

Relief flooded through her. So he hadn't entirely forgotten her! 'Of course I've changed! I was only sixteen
when you went off to Australia to get married.'

Pierre was smiling now, displaying the firm white teeth
she'd so admired when she looked up to him as a child.

'I should have recognised your long auburn hair and
those flashing green eyes! I remember my mother was
always remarking what a pretty child you were.'

Jacky swallowed hard. A pretty child she may have
been but Pierre only had eyes for girls much older than
she was.

'But your surname, Manson?' Pierre queried. 'Are you married?'

'I was married…but we…er…we divorced. I kept the surname because I was married when I qualified as a doctor and I've never got around to changing back to my maiden name.'

'I remember you were the only child in the village with an English surname. Your father was English and your mother was French, as I recall. Shaftesbury was such an unusual name in France.'

Jacky gave a wry smile. 'When I was small some of my little friends found it difficult to say. Even my teacher in the *école primaire* had a problem. But since my divorce I've sometimes wondered if I should get rid of my married name and make a clean break with that…difficult time in my life.'

'It's always hard to move on, isn't it?' Pierre said.

Jacky noticed that his voice was low and husky and held a hint of sadness. 'Almost impossible,' she agreed.

Pierre was holding her gaze and she enjoyed the feeling of sharing an intimate moment with him. She knew nothing of what had happened to him since he'd left Normandy when she'd been sixteen. He must have been twenty-five then. She'd always imagined him happily married to the beautiful fellow medical student he'd brought home to the village one time. So how come his eyes conveyed a deep sadness? He was still charming, handsome and confident, but he no longer had that carefree manner that had been so typical of him.

His eyes clouded over and she could no longer interpret his enigmatic expression.

'Life can be full of surprises,' he said slowly. 'Some of them very disturbing.'

She looked away, feeling her heart beginning to beat a little too fast.

Was Pierre trying to move on from some unpleasant happening, as she was? She was constantly trying to look towards the future in a positive way. Maybe she should take her maiden name again. Two years on from that heart-rending divorce, Jacky wondered briefly if it would help the healing process to discard all the relics from the past. After all, she had nothing of value to hang on to from the marriage…except… If only her precious baby had survived, then perhaps she…

Marcel gave a discreet cough. 'So, you two knew each other a long time ago?'

'Jacqueline was only a child when I last saw her.' Pierre Mellanger gave a boyish grin. 'A very precocious child, as I recall. We lived near each other in Normandy, in a small village on the coast near Mont Saint Michel, and sometimes Jacqueline and her young friends would follow me around, especially if I had a girlfriend with me.'

Jacky was regaining her composure as the memories flooded back. 'You were so much older than we were. Whenever you came home from medical school in Paris we all wanted to find out what it was like to live in the big city. But you were much too sophisticated to talk to us.'

Pierre sighed. 'I couldn't wait to escape from the countryside in those days. Now I'm glad to get away from the bright lights of Paris to live by the sea in a more rural area of France again. And St Martin sur mer reminds me of the village where I was born. I can enjoy a much healthier lifestyle here.'

Through the open window Pierre caught a glimpse of the sea and felt a surge of energy running through him. Since arriving in St Martin from Paris yesterday evening he'd already felt that this might be the environment where the healing process could be accelerated. The place where the problems in his life would become easier to cope with.

He glanced across at Jacky. Now that he'd spent time talking to her, it wasn't difficult to believe that this tall, slender, beautiful woman was the pretty, carefree child who'd run around the village laughing and joking with her many friends.

She'd been extremely popular as a child, Pierre remembered. A leader amongst the village children, vibrant, active and full of energy. The sort of girl who'd stood out from the crowd. She seemed to have undergone something of a personality change. There was a distinct air of vulnerability about her. It was as if she was expecting to be dealt another blow to her self-esteem.

But he couldn't help admitting to himself that, in spite of the difficult situation in which he was now entrenched, he found this grown-up version of little Jacky extremely attractive. He remembered seeing Jacky when she'd been sixteen—just before he'd gone out to Australia—and thinking how stunning she was. But by then he had been a twenty-five-year-old, soon-to-be-married man who'd known he shouldn't allow himself to admire the opposite sex. But there had been no harm in looking at her.

'I thought you were still in Australia,' Jacky said, admitting to herself that if she'd known there had been the slightest chance of meeting up with Pierre during her medical work she wouldn't have risked coming back to France. Young love when it's unrequited was a difficult emotion to survive. She'd hoped the ache would go away, but it never had. She admitted unwillingly that it was still there now.

'France will always be home,' Pierre said, his voice

suddenly full of undisguised emotion. 'When life becomes difficult…' His voice trailed away.

Marcel put a hand on Pierre's arm. 'I've known Pierre since we were medical students in Paris,' he interjected quickly. 'We both went out to Australia soon after we qualified to work in a hospital in Sydney.'

'Young men, longing to see the world!' Pierre said, his firm voice showing that his momentary loss of control had passed. 'But when life gets tough, it's better to be amongst your compatriots. Isn't that so, Marcel?'

Marcel nodded. 'That's why we both returned to France.' He turned to Jacky. 'At different times and for different reasons.' He paused. 'But let's get back to business. I'm handing over my job to Pierre and moving upstairs to take over as surgical consultant this morning.'

'You've kept this very quiet, Marcel,' Jacky said. 'Why all the secrecy? I thought you were happy in Urgences.'

Marcel shrugged. 'I am…I mean, I was. But surgery has always been where I feel most fulfilled. When Victor Ramond told me he was going to retire he suggested I might like to apply for the post. Victor told me he didn't want anyone to know he was going until the actual day. The hospital board already had a list of candidates who applied a year ago when Victor changed his mind about retiring early. They simply added me to the list.'

'So that was why everything was kept quiet this time, I suppose,' Jacky said. 'To make sure dear old Victor wouldn't change his mind again.'

She turned to look at Pierre, feeling the familiar rush of excitement as she looked up into his handsome face. Why, oh, why was she still suffering from this childish crush which was permanently doomed to be unrequited? Especially now. Even if Pierre showed an interest in her, she couldn't possibly give in to her emotions.

'Pierre, did Marcel contact you about taking over his post in Urgences?'

'Yes. It came exactly at the right time when I needed...I needed to get away from Paris. There were other candidates, of course, but I suspect Marcel's first-class reference swung the interview panel in my favour.'

'You were the best man for the job,' Marcel put in firmly. 'It's as simple as that. It also helps that we've been friends and colleagues for a long time and know all each other's secrets.'

'Strange, meeting up with old friends like this,' Pierre said quietly. 'I was hoping that when I left Paris—'

'*Excusez-moi, Pierre.*' Marcel pressed the intercom switch which had been buzzing for several seconds. '*Oui?*' He was listening intently. '*J'arrive tout de suite.*'

Marcel stood up. 'There's an emergency. We must all go to Urgences at once. A tourist boat has capsized. The paramedics are bringing in the casualties. I can stay to help for an hour, after which I'm due in Theatre.'

In an instant all three doctors were back into strictly professional mode as they hurried along the corridor. Memories and reminiscences were forgotten as they concentrated all their energy and expertise into saving their patients.

The survivors were being wheeled in on trolleys as the three of them arrived in the main reception area of Urgences. Sister Marie Bezier was quickly advised about the change of consultant. She welcomed Pierre as she took him along to examine one of the victims.

Extra doctors were arriving as the survivors were being wheeled in. Jacky was immediately called upon to examine an elderly lady who'd been taken into a cubicle and placed on the examination couch. The patient looked up at Jacky with imploring eyes. *'Ma jambe, c'est cassé, docteur?'*

Looking down at the unnatural angle of her patient's leg, it was obvious that, yes, the leg was broken.

Jacky took hold of her patient's hand. 'We're going to X-ray your leg but I think it's broken. The X-ray will tell us the extent of the damage, Madame…' She was glancing down at the notes for the lady's name.

'Please, call me Marguerite.'

'Mais oui, bien sûr, Marguerite. And you must call me Jacky or Jacqueline, *comme vous voulez.'*

'Ah, moi, je préfere Jacqueline. C'est le nom de ma fille. Jacqueline est…'

As Jacky continued her preliminary examination, her elderly patient chatted about her daughter Jacqueline and her other children and grandchildren. Jacky always made a point of gaining the confidence of her patients as soon as possible. Especially the older ones. She kept one ear on what her patient was saying as she scanned the notes made by the paramedic who'd gone out in the rescue boat to help the survivors after their pleasure boat had sunk.

She learned that Marguerite Formentier, aged seventy-five, had been one of the lucky ones who had been given a life jacket minutes before the boat had sunk. But as she'd tried to jump into the water she'd banged herself against the side of the boat and hurt the top of her right leg. Already suffering from osteoporosis, her fragile bone had fractured.

As she accompanied her patient to the adjoining X-ray room Jacky asked Marguerite what had happened.

'Oh, we were all enjoying our day out when suddenly there was a terrible cracking sound. We were only metres away from the little island where we were going to picnic when the boat ran aground on some rocks. The boat started filling with water. Some of the younger people started jumping overboard but I'm not as agile as I used to be so I just sat there praying somebody would help me.'

'And fortunately your prayers were answered,' Jacky said as she motioned to the radiologist exactly where she wanted the X-ray to be directed.

'There was one older couple I'd been talking to—they could have been older than me, I think. They held hands and jumped into the sea. I never found out what happened to them because I didn't see them again.'

'Keep very still now, Marguerite,' the radiologist said.

In a couple of minutes Jacky was examining the X-ray plates. She turned back to explain what would happen next to her patient.

'Marguerite, you've broken the end of your leg where it fits into the hip socket, here at the top,' she told her gently.

'You mean the femur, don't you? I used to be a nurse so you can tell me how bad it is.'

'Well, the head of the femur has been fractured and dislocated from the acetabulum. You'll probably need a prosthesis because of the extent of the damage.'

Marguerite shrugged. '*Eh bien*, I think my hip was getting a bit loose anyway. I was planning to go and see my doctor soon to discuss a hip replacement. So getting shipwrecked just moved the process on a bit more quickly, didn't it?'

Jacky smiled. 'I wish all my patients were as positive as you, Marguerite. Now, I'm going to have you transferred to the preliminary orthopaedic unit, which is just along the corridor. You'll be seen there as soon as possible by one of the orthopaedic doctors who'll decide when they can take you into the operating theatre.'

'*Merci beaucoup*, Jacqueline. You have been so kind. Will you come to see me when I'm in Orthopaedics?'

'Of course I will. I like to keep up with what's happening to all my patients who're admitted.'

Back in the main reception area a small boy was being wheeled in.

'Dominic, age two. Just arrived here, Doctor,' the paramedic told her. 'Been in the water too long, I think. A scuba diver went down and found him on the seabed, trapped under a rock.' He lowered his voice. 'Not much hope, I'm afraid. I can't find a pulse and he isn't breathing. We've tried mouth-to-mouth resuscitation and everything else, but he's not responding.'

Jacky had the boy moved swiftly into a cubicle, assigning a nurse to take care of the accompanying parents in an adjoining cubicle. Having dived repeatedly to look for their son, who'd been washed overboard, they were hysterical when the professional scuba diver arrived. They had no outward injuries but Jacky instructed the nurse to treat them for intense shock and call for help if their condition didn't improve.

Quickly, she turned her attention to the tiny lifeless form beneath the blanket. The small white face above the blanket looked somehow ethereal and angelic. The expression was one of calm...already other-worldly. Jacky drew in her breath as she tried to stay completely professional.

'How long was the boy in the water?' she asked the paramedic.

'Probably half an hour at least. He was freezing cold when the diver brought him up.'

Pierre came in at the moment when the paramedic was describing the boy's rescue. 'You say he was freezing cold? With a child as young as this there's still a chance.'

Jacky had already connected little Dominic to the monitor. They both glanced at the temperature reading. Incredibly low! Jacky had never seen a patient with such a low temperature. But she remembered a textbook case where a young boy had survived drowning precisely because his body temperature had been cooled down.

She looked up at Pierre. 'Are you thinking what I'm thinking, that because Dominic's temperature is barely above freezing his chances of survival have increased?'

Pierre nodded. 'I had a case like this in Australia once during the winter. Having plunged down to the sea bed, where it was exceptionally cold, his metabolism was slowed down, and most importantly his brain needed little oxygen. We must try to raise the body temperature, but very, very slowly. I'm not going to give up on him until his body is nearing normal temperature.'

'Warm fluids are needed,' Jacky said, remembering the textbook case from her medical training.

'I'll catheterise him and wash out the bladder with warm sterile water,' Pierre said, before calling over one of the nurses to prepare a dressings trolley with the necessary instruments.

'I'll put a gastric tube down and wash out Dominic's stomach,' Jacky said.

Pierre glanced around the cubicle. 'Nurse, have you got one of those special blankets that blow hot air onto the patient?'

'I'll ask Sister Marie.' The nurse pushed the prepared dressings trolley towards Pierre, before hurrying away to find the special blanket.

After working on the little boy for what seemed an eternity, Jacky pointed to the monitor. 'Look! There's a faint, slow pulse coming through.'

She put her hand to the patient's wrist. At first she

could feel nothing except cold lifeless flesh, but then she detected the merest hint of a pulse.

'I'll start massaging his heart,' Pierre said as once more he leaned across his little patient.

Minutes, then hours went by as Pierre and Jacky struggled to revive the little boy. The distraught parents, who'd been advised that his chances of survival were slim, had been taken to the preliminary medical unit where they could be cared for until the outcome of the resuscitation attempt was known.

After four hours Jacky was beginning to feel the strain. She'd become intensely fond of this seemingly lifeless boy. She looked across at Pierre.

'I'll check his reaction to light again,' she said, trying to sound hopeful. All her previous attempts had been unsuccessful.

She picked up her ophthalmoscope and pressed it on. Lifting one tiny eyelid, she shone a pinprick of light into the eye. For one exciting moment she held her breath.

'He's reacting! The pupil reacted. I know it did. Pierre, come and check it out.'

Pierre took the ophthalmoscope and bent over the patient. Moments later he raised himself. 'You're right, Jacky!'

His voice conveyed his excitement and relief. 'His chances of life are growing by the minute. Isn't that wonderful!'

He turned round, the ophthalmoscope still clutched in his hand, and threw his arms around Jacky. 'We mustn't give up until…'

Pierre's excitement was infectious. Jacky smiled up into his eyes. The feel of his arms as he hugged her was, oh, so good…but, oh, so terribly disturbing. Had Pierre any idea what his unexpected embrace was doing to her?

Pierre, looking down at the beautiful young woman in his arms, checked his enthusiasm and dropped his arms to his sides. He wasn't usually so demonstrative. He didn't know what had come over him. Yes, there was a real excuse for getting excited like this, but Jacky might misconstrue his motives and that would be disastrous.

He turned back to his patient and listened to his chest with his stethoscope. 'There's a definite heartbeat now…getting stronger all the time…'

'Temperature's almost back to normal,' Jacky said as she checked the monitor once more.

'His breathing is getting steadier. I think he's trying to… He…he's opening his eyes…'

Jacky took hold of little Dominic's hand as she watched the fluttering of the tiny eyelids. The little boy whimpered, then made a spluttering sound before uttering one feeble plaintive word. *'Maman.'*

Jacky was holding back her tears as she leaned over her patient. *'Je vais chercher maman pour toi, Dominic. Maman will come to see you soon.'*

'Et papa?'

'Papa aussi,' Jacky reassured him.

She turned to look at Pierre. *'C'est un miracle.'*

Pierre noticed Jacky's eyes were swimming with tears. He wanted so much to lean forward and hug her again but he resisted the temptation. The only time he'd seen her cry had been when she'd fallen over whilst playing with her friends amongst the slippery rocks on the beach near the village. She must have been about five.

He'd been kicking a football about with a couple of friends nearby and when he'd heard her scream out in pain, he'd gone to her rescue. There had been blood streaming from the cut in her leg and he'd torn off the bottom of his shirt, applied a pressure bandage and carried her to his father's surgery in the village.

The little girl had been as light as a feather and he had been a tall, strong fourteen-year-old so carrying her hadn't been a problem to him. She'd put her tiny arms around his neck, he remembered, and clung to him. He'd found it very touching, her complete trust that he would know what to do.

He also remembered that his mother hadn't entirely approved of the Shaftesbury parents. Jacky's mother had been too flamboyant and her father too unconventional to be accepted by the old-fashioned villagers, who were mostly rooted in the past. But when his mother had seen Pierre walking up the path towards the surgery she'd hurried across to give her husband a hand. As a trained nurse his mother was always there to assist her husband when he needed her.

Young Jacky had been duly stitched up. Pierre remembered how brave the little girl had been once she'd got over the initial shock. And one of the bonbons that his father always kept in the drawer of his desk had helped to stem the flow of tears. Pierre was sure that this sophisticated doctor wouldn't remember how she'd clung to his hand as his father had applied the local anaesthetic to the wound on her leg. He must have been just one of the faceless big boys, light years older than she had been in those days.

'Yes, Dominic's revival is a miracle,' Pierre said solemnly as he leaned across their small patient towards Jacky. 'He was technically dead for some considerable time. I'm going to call the cardiac team again. They gave up on him soon after he arrived. I think everybody thought we were mad to believe we could revive him.'

Jacky gave a relieved smile. 'We've got cause to celebrate, don't you think, because—'

She broke off. The way she'd phrased it in French had made it sound as if she'd been suggesting they go out and have a drink or something. That wasn't what she had meant at all, although it was a very tempting idea.

Pierre's eyes registered his surprise. 'Yes, I agree, I think we should celebrate when we go off duty,' he said, slowly. 'Perhaps…'

'Pierre, I didn't mean it in that way, I—' She broke off to squeeze her little patient's hand and utter soothing words of comfort. She was rewarded with Dominic's attempt at a smile and a few more mostly incoherent words.

'I think we should celebrate tonight,' Pierre said. 'I'll need to make some arrangements for…'

A doctor from the intensive care unit and one from the cardiac team came into the cubicle and Pierre broke off so that they could all join in the discussion about treatment.

After Jacky and Pierre had handed over their precious patient there was no time to reopen the subject of celebration as they were both required back in the main reception area to deal with the final patients from the boat disaster who hadn't yet been treated.

Jacky found herself confronted by an elderly man who, miraculously, had survived serious injury when he'd jumped into the water. His wife, who had just been brought in, was barely alive. Jacky rated her chances of survival as very slim.

Her husband was very positive about the heartbreaking situation as he sat on a chair at the side of the cubicle.

'I took hold of Anne-Marie's hand and told her to jump with me when the boat started going down,' he said in a quavering voice. 'She let go of my hand in the water and then somebody pulled me up into the rescue boat. I kept telling them my wife was still in the water and a kind man in a diving suit went to look for her. They found her floating on the surface a little while ago. She was still breathing and they tried to revive her. Do you think there's any chance, Doctor, that you can…?'

The elderly man's voice choked and he passed an old wrinkled hand over his face.

Jacky deduced that this might be the couple that Marguerite had spoken about. In the short time that she'd been helping the resuscitation team she'd realised that they were fighting a losing battle with Anne-Marie. As all signs of life had faded away, they had just agreed to abandon the attempt.

'*Je suis desolée, monsieur.* I'm so sorry, but there is nothing more we can do for your wife. We've tried everything and…'

As the man raised his tear-filled eyes towards the young doctor he thought how pretty she was…just like his wonderful Anne-Marie had been.

'It's all right, Doctor. I understand… Anne-Marie and I have had a good life so it's…it's time to say goodbye now.'

The old man seemed to have aged as he began to struggle to his feet. Jacky put an arm round his back and helped him up. He attempted a weak smile before walking slowly over to where the lifeless body of his wife was now covered with a white sheet. For a second he held himself erect and dignified, looking down on the love of his life before leaning down to kiss her gently on the side of her white cheek.

'*Au revoir, chérie,*' he whispered. '*À bientôt.*'

Jacky swallowed the lump in her throat, again experiencing the need to hold back the tears, this time tears of sadness. Listening to the old man whispering that he would see his wife soon was almost too much to bear. As a doctor she should be immune to all the emotions experienced in her medical work. But she realised that only a robot could work with people as she did and remain immune to the excruciating human sadness that went with the job.

Putting an arm around the old man, she led him gently away. His eyes were now dry and he was stoical in his grief.

'We'd like you to spend the night here in the hospital, *monsieur*,' she said gently. 'We need to check out your general health before we can discharge you. Have you got any relatives we should inform about…?'

'Would you phone my eldest daughter? I can't remember her number and I've lost my wallet in the sea somewhere. She'll be in the phone book if you could have a look for me. I—'

'I'll sort this out for you, Jacky,' Sister Marie said, coming quietly across the main reception area. 'There's a patient in cubicle four with a leg wound, waiting to be seen by a doctor. I think that's the last of the survivors to be treated.'

Jacky handed over responsibility of her patient, telling him that Marie was going to take care of him. Then she headed off for her next assignment.

By the time she'd sutured the deep wound on her next patient's leg it was an hour later than the time she should have gone off duty. Coming out of the cubicle, she ran a hand over her hair, which she'd tied up on the top of her head in a tight knot as soon as she'd started working.

'Time you were off duty, Jacky,' Marie said, coming

across the reception area. 'Everything is under control at last. I'll soon be handing over to the night staff.'

'What about you? Haven't you been here all day?'

Marie smiled. 'I had a couple of hours off in the middle of the day and handed over to my deputy. You look very tired, Jacky.'

'I'll be OK.'

Jacky looked around the quiet reception area where the newly arrived non-urgent patients were waiting to be treated by the night staff. Difficult to believe that this was the area that had resembled a war zone earlier in the day.

As she walked out through the swing doors that led to the staff cloakrooms she put her hand up to her hair and loosened the knot. Her hair came tumbling down to her shoulders and she felt a sense of relief. This was always the signal that her working day was finished.

'That's how I remember you when you were small.'

She turned around at the sound of Pierre's voice. She was surprised to hear that he was speaking to her in English. Well, he had spent some time in Australia, she remembered. He was hurrying down the corridor behind her, his long legs covering the ground at an alarming speed. She stood still until he came alongside her.

'I wanted to catch you before you went off,' he said, putting a hand on her arm as if making the point that he didn't want her to start walking off again. 'I'm going to have to postpone our celebration because—'

'Pierre, I really didn't mean that—'

'Oh, but I did! I insist we celebrate soon, but not to-night.'

'Pierre, I wasn't thinking. I mean, your wife must come with us and—'

'I'm sorry. I should have told you.' His happy expression changed. 'My wife died.'

'I'm so sorry.' Her voice was full of emotion. What else could she say as she remembered the beautiful young woman she'd seen with Pierre all those years ago. They had seemed so much in love.

Instinctively she moved closer to him, wanting to give him some comfort other than mere words. But almost as soon as she moved she stepped back again. Physical comfort from a woman who'd adored him from afar for as long as she could remember wasn't a good idea and would only fan the flames of her unrequited devotion.

'How long ago is it since you lost your wife?' she asked gently.

His eyes remained dry but Jacky could see the pain behind his brave façade.

'Five years ago. I should be over it by now but…some things in life take a long time to heal.'

'I know,' she said quietly, as the trauma surrounding her own devastating loss returned to haunt her again.

'I have to stay on here for another couple of hours to get to grips with the administration of the department. Marcel has agreed to come down when he's finished in Theatre to explain what happens here. He meant to do this during the day but we were both too busy.'

'You can say that again!' Jacky said lightly. 'Oh, it's so nice to be speaking English again. Do you know, Pierre, I do believe that along with your French accent you have a slight Australian accent.'

He gave her a wry grin. 'Not surprising after all the years I spent there. But it seems strange to talk to you in English. You always spoke French when you were a child.'

'My mother insisted on it, even though she had to allow my father to chat to me in English occasionally.'

'Hey, we've got such a lot of catching up to do! Let's

go out for a meal some time, my treat—no, I insist. How are you fixed tomorrow? I'll arrange we both go off duty around the same time.'

She smiled up at him. 'I'd enjoy that. Yes, I'll clear my social diary—only joking, there's very little in there apart from work.'

Pierre laughed. 'We've only just arrived here so I know my social diary is completely empty.' He leaned forward and took a strand of her long auburn hair between his fingers.

'You know, your hair is rather like spun gold,' he said, softly. 'As a child I read this story about a princess whose hair was like spun gold. I didn't believe that hair could be like that, but when I was older and I used to see you running about in the village with your long hair streaming behind you, I decided that was what the writer had meant.'

Jacky swallowed hard. 'I didn't know you even noticed me.'

'Oh, yes…I noticed you. You were very…distinctive and…very sweet.' He lowered his head and kissed her on the side of the cheek. 'Good night, Jacky.'

She moved in the opposite direction from Pierre as he went back the way he'd come. But at the corner of the corridor she turned to watch him, realising that nothing had changed as far as she was concerned. She still found Pierre infinitely exciting.

She shivered as she moved away. It would be so hard to fight her real feelings if ever she found herself in an intimate situation with Pierre. But from the expression in Pierre's eyes when he'd spoken of his dead wife it looked as if he was still grieving for the love of his life.

CHAPTER TWO

THROUGHOUT the next day, as Jacky worked in Urgences she was constantly meeting or working with Pierre. He made a point of reminding her that they were going out together that evening.

As if she needed reminding! She'd found it difficult to sleep during the night. It was as if her teenage crush on Pierre had been revived with full force and her impossible teenage emotions along with it! Teenage emotions were difficult enough to handle when you were a teenager. She should have learned how to cope now that she was a twenty-nine-year-old divorcée who had briefly been a mother. Her life experience should have hardened her. But deep down she felt as excited as if she were going out on her very first date.

In between treating new patients for a variety of injuries she made time to check on some of the patients from the boat disaster. Dominic, the toddler who'd defied all the odds by literally returning from the dead was being treated with round-the-clock specialist medical care. His brain had been scanned and declared unharmed.

Jacky was relieved to hear this, as were the other doctors involved in the case. This was always the prime concern with a patient who had been unconscious for a long period of time. Once again, Jacky felt his recovery had been a miracle.

Somebody had leaked the story of Dominic's miraculous revival to the press. Consequently, Jacky and Pierre reluctantly agreed to be photographed in the main reception area. Pierre had checked with Marcel to see what he thought of the idea. Marcel had said there was no reason why the general public shouldn't hear about a success story.

'The next time somebody feels like writing to the press about having to wait too long to be seen in Urgences, they might remember we do sometimes perform miracles. But don't let them anywhere near young Dominic. They'll have to wait until he goes home for a shot of the miracle boy—assuming his parents are willing.'

So Jacky found herself standing next to Pierre in the requisite clean white coat with her stethoscope slung round her neck in the centre of the main reception area.

'We've only got a few minutes to spare,' Pierre told the two photographers. 'So if you could be as quick as—'

'Stand a bit closer to the lovely lady doctor,' one photographer said, coming forward to set the scene for his picture.

The young man from the local paper had got the full story from his girlfriend who was a nurse. He was anxious to get into print before the national papers. The hospital was always reticent about their patients so he'd been very lucky to be tipped off.

His assistant turned to Jacky. 'Do you think you could let your hair down, docteur? It's such a lovely colour and our readers will...'

Jacky groaned inwardly as she wrested the clasp from her hair.

'*Merci beaucoup, docteur*... Yes, that's better... Now, a big smile.'

'What a handsome couple!' one of the nurses remarked as she walked past, pushing a trolley.

Jacky felt suddenly embarrassed by all the attention they were getting. She was also intensely aware of Pierre standing close beside her. She could feel the heat from his body. Very disturbing! She continued to smile but behind the smile she was intensely unnerved.

'We'll have to stop now,' Pierre said firmly. 'I'm in the middle of—'

'We'll have that in the evening paper tonight, *docteur*,' the photographer said. 'I'll make sure we send you a few copies.'

Pierre looked at Jacky. 'Well, that will be something to look forward to, won't it?' he said wryly.

Jacky grinned. 'Can't wait.'

'By the time we get to the restaurant we'll be celebrities. They'll give us the best table and ask for our autographs,' Pierre quipped.

'I'll take my pen,' Jacky said solemnly.

She turned to go back to the patient she'd left in X-Ray under the care of a nurse. The X-rays of her patient's arm would be ready for her to examine now and she'd be able to make a decision on his treatment.

There were no further interruptions to her work for the rest of the day and it looked as if she would get off duty on time. Some time towards the end of the afternoon she found time to go and see Marguerite, her fractured femur and dislocation of hip patient who'd been moved to the orthopaedic ward after her operation the previous evening.

Propped against her pillows, the elderly lady smiled when Jacky arrived.

'I'm absolutely fine,' Marguerite told Jacky when she enquired. 'They're giving me pills so I don't feel any pain and I've got my new hip, haven't I? The lengths to which some people will go so that they can jump the hospital waiting list!'

Jacky laughed. 'We'll soon have you moving around again, Marguerite.'

'I hope so.'

* * *

As she was clearing up after treating her final patient in Urgences, Pierre came up to say that he was ready to go off duty. He'd handed over to his deputy so as soon as she could finish off they could leave together.

'We'll take my car,' he told her.

'That's a good idea because I haven't got one. Apart from the expense of buying and running a car, parking is difficult in the narrow road where I live. Besides, I'm only minutes from the hospital, so why would I need a car?'

'To get out into the lovely countryside around here? Don't you ever long to get away from the hospital area?'

He was looking down at her with the expressive dark eyes that she remembered so well from the time she'd been close up to him as a child. It might have been that time she'd hurt her leg. She couldn't really remember. But she knew that she'd looked into his eyes as a child at some time and been absolutely smitten!

Yes, now she remembered. It had been the time she'd slipped on the rocks and had needed stitches in her leg from Pierre's dad at his surgery. Pierre had carried her there, and even though her leg had been hurting she'd felt safe and comforted in his arms.

'I walk on the beach when I need to get away,' she said quickly.

'Well, let's get away now. I've made a reservation at a small restaurant that Marcel recommended to me. It's out of town, up in the hills somewhere. I've got it marked on my map. Are you any good at navigation?'

Jacky pushed the treatment trolley against the wall and began to wash her hands. 'I'll give it a try. It's not as if we're going far, is it?'

He was standing close behind her. She could feel his warm breath on the back of her neck. She'd rewound her hair into its working time knot as soon as the photographer had finished his session with them. Deftly, Pierre undid the clasp holding it in place and the long auburn strands fell down to her shoulders again. She swung round.

'What is it with you men that you're always trying to make me let my hair down?'

Pierre raised an eyebrow. 'It makes you look more approachable…more…' He lowered his voice to a husky whisper. 'More sexy…'

He'd been standing very close but now he moved away quickly. As he headed for the door he was wishing he hadn't made that last remark. But standing close to Jacky just now, it had almost been as if the difficult years in between had been a figment of his imagination. He'd been taken right back to the last time he'd had a glimpse of a beautiful sixteen-year-old girl and had realised that the pretty young girl from the village had grown up.

But it was too late now. He had to hold himself in control and not give Jacky the wrong idea. He'd vowed to stay true to Liliane for ever. At the very least he owed her complete loyalty in return for the great sacrifice she'd made, he thought with a pang of guilt.

An occasional non-emotional fling with someone was acceptable, but he instinctively knew that any liaison with Jacky would mean too much to him. His feelings for her were becoming stronger every time they worked together.

'Come to my office as soon as you're ready,' Pierre said brusquely as he swung out through the door.

Jacky stared after him. She couldn't think why his mood had changed so abruptly. He'd actually seemed so friendly…well, more than friendly.

She told herself it didn't matter. She was used to it where Pierre was concerned. She'd go out for the evening and enjoy herself with him…as a friend from the past. End of story.

In the changing room she had a quick shower and put on fresh clothes. She'd brought the white linen trousers and black cotton top with the broderie anglaise neckline, she'd bought in Le Touquet last week. The white linen jacket she'd worn when walking here this morning teamed up with it very well. It had been a warm June day but the evening might turn out to be chilly.

A little make-up, not too much, but her green eyes always looked better if she used mascara. Hmm… She stared at herself in the mirror. Why was she taking such trouble when she planned to remain just a friend to Pierre?

The tragedy of her past had put paid to anything more than good friendship. That's what her head was telling her, but her heart was reacting in a completely different…and extremely dangerous way.

Pierre stood up when she went into his office. His smile was welcoming but cool. He moved around his desk, picking up his mobile which had just started to ring.

'Oui? Ah, Nadine, qu'est-ce qu'il y a? Oui, d'accord, j'arrive.'

He cut the connection. 'I'll have to call in at the house. A small…a small problem.'

Jacky was curious. Who was Nadine? She'd been able to hear a woman's high-pitched voice when Pierre was on the phone, a woman who'd sounded upset about something.

As they walked out into the corridor together, Marcel came hurrying along to meet them. He thrust a couple of copies of the evening paper into Pierre's hand.

'These have just arrived, Pierre. Don't you two look fantastic on the front page? It says, ''Handsome Docteur

Pierre and the lovely Docteur Jacqueline performed a miracle yesterday when—'''

Pierre groaned. 'Thank you Marcel. I'll read it later.' He turned to Jacky. 'Here's yours. Hope you've got your pen for the autographs tonight.'

Jacky looked down at the picture of the two of them smiling into the camera.

'A good advertisement for the hospital, showing that sometimes we can make a difference to the lives of the people around here,' Marcel said. 'Where are the two of you heading off to tonight?'

'We're going to that restaurant you recommended.'

'Ah, oui, c'est excellent!' Marcel looked from one to the other of them. 'Well, don't let me delay you. You must come and have supper with us one evening when you're both free. Debbie would love to see you. She loves to see friends from the hospital.'

'I'm looking forward to seeing Debbie again later this week during my off-duty,' Jacky said.

Marcel smiled as he turned to Pierre. 'Jacky is like one of the family now. She and Debbie became firm friends when they talked over the phone and exchanged messages over the internet before Jacky started working here. And then when Jacky arrived here in March, three months before our baby was due, she was an invaluable help to Debbie as they worked together.'

Jacky smiled happily. 'I was so thrilled last December when Debbie phoned to invite me to your wedding, Marcel. It was such a beautiful wedding, just before Christmas. Debbie looked stunning in her beautiful wedding gown with your lovely little stepdaughter as bridesmaid.'

'You have a stepdaughter?' Pierre said.

'Emma is Debbie's daughter from her previous relationship but she feels more like my own daughter. I've legally adopted her now,' Marcel said proudly. 'She's seven years old…going on seventeen! She simply adores her baby brother and thinks the world revolves around him. She dashes in from school every day and…'

Marcel broke off with a sheepish grin. 'But I must be boring you, playing the proud father.'

'*Pas du tout.* Not at all,' Pierre said. 'How old is your baby son?'

'Eight weeks.'

'He's absolutely gorgeous!' Jacky interjected. 'It's wonderful to see Debbie so happy. She's a brilliant mother, so calm all the time. No wonder little Thiery is such a good baby.'

'I look forward to meeting Debbie. Well, we must be off,' Pierre said, putting his hand lightly on Jacky's back.

'*Bonne soirée!*' Marcel said.

Pierre smiled. '*Merci.*'

As Marcel watched his two colleagues walking away he felt pleased to see how well they were getting on together. In fact, if he hadn't known Pierre better, he would have thought there was a budding romance there. But knowing the problems that Pierre still had to surmount, Marcel doubted that Jacky and Pierre would ever progress beyond being good friends. They had known each other a long time ago and this had obviously created an immediate bond between them. But as far as a serious romance went, that was most probably out of the question.

Marcel sighed as he walked in the other direction. It was a pity there seemed very little hope of them becoming a real couple because they looked so good together. And Pierre was starved of real love and affection. Someone like Jacky would have made all the difference to his life.

Just like his wonderful wife Debbie had transformed

his own life. He mustn't interfere in Pierre's life. But if ever he was asked for his advice, knowing what he did about Pierre's marriage to Liliane, he might be able to make a difference to the outcome…

Jacky fastened her seat belt and sank back against the deeply comfortable passenger seat.

She smiled. 'Nice car!' she said in English.

'I was lucky to get it. One of the doctors at my hospital in Paris was selling it because his wife is having a baby and didn't like the idea of driving around in a sports car. It's only a year old. I drove down from Paris a couple of days ago and it handled like a dream.'

Pierre started the engine and the car purred out through the gates onto the main road.

'I live up the hill, on the same road as Marcel. When I was appointed I asked him to let me know if there were any houses for sale in this area. Again, I was very lucky to find one. I came over once from Paris to view it and arranged to buy it at once.'

Jacky looked out as Pierre, reducing his speed, drove at a more sedate pace along the tree-lined road that led towards his house. The large houses were well spaced out on the top side of the road and there were no buildings on the lower side.

'You must have a fabulous view from your house!' Jacky said, as she looked out over the sea.

'That was one of the things that drew me to the house,' Pierre said. 'The view and the large garden surrounding it which is so good for—' He broke off in mid-sentence.

'It's always a good idea to have a large garden,' he finished off hurriedly.

Jacky was curious. Why did she often have the feeling when she was with Pierre that he was hiding something?

'So, do you enjoy gardening, Pierre?'

He hesitated. 'Sometimes.'

Jacky had no idea why his animated mood had suddenly changed. She looked down at the spectacular view.

Yachts and pleasure boats were bobbing on the sparkling water where the twilight colours were deepening into red and gold. There were still some people on the beach taking an evening stroll, their tiny figures below her looking like matchstick men.

'Here we are,' Pierre said, as he drove into a wide sweeping gravel drive, drawing to a halt in front of an imposing oak, brass-studded door.

The door opened almost immediately and a tall young woman, probably in her early twenties, came out onto the front step. She was wearing jeans and a white T-shirt and seemed very pleased that Pierre had arrived.

Pierre leapt over the driver's side of the car without opening the door.

'I'll be back in a couple of minutes,' he called, leaving Jacky wondering why he wasn't inviting her inside.

He disappeared into the house, the woman following closely behind. Who was she? Jacky sat in the car feeling decidedly unwelcome. This was totally out of character with the hospitable Pierre she thought she knew…and a little too mysterious for her liking!

She stared up at the trees overhanging the drive. At least she was sitting in a sports car so she could appreciate the scent of the roses that bordered the drive. And Pierre had promised not to be long, so…

She could hear a child shouting somewhere upstairs…the sounds coming through the open window. This was definitely a young, highly vociferous child, and now she could hear Pierre speaking firmly but in very soothing tones. The child calmed down. She could hear the sound of laughter, Pierre's, the child's and the lighter tones of a woman.

If it was Pierre's child, as now seemed highly probable, why hadn't he told her?

Now there were only the sounds of the woman talking to the child. Jacky glanced at her watch. It was only five minutes since Pierre had gone inside. She decided to climb out. Opening the passenger door, she stretched her long legs and climbed out onto the crunchy gravel. One of the tiny stones slipped inside her sandal. She bent down to extricate it just as the door opened and Pierre came out.

She felt something akin to guilt at having got out when she'd been told to wait in the car. She straightened up, wondering, irrationally, if she would be reprimanded for stepping onto the drive uninvited. Pierre swiftly reached the car. There was a careworn expression on his face and his mouth was set in a straight line.

'I'm sorry to keep you waiting,' he said quietly, holding open the passenger door so that she could get back inside.

Was he going to tell her about the child? She glanced across but saw that his thoughts seemed to be elsewhere as he restarted the car and drove off down the drive towards the road. Not until they'd turned the corner and were heading upwards towards the open hills did Jacky sense that he'd relaxed again. She wanted so much to ask him about who lived in the house with him. Was the child his? If so, why hadn't he told her? Perhaps it belonged to the woman.

But who was the woman? Pierre was an only child so she couldn't be his sister. And his wife was dead. Could she be his girlfriend? Most unlikely! What girlfriend would watch her husband driving away for a date with another woman?

She mustn't pry. Pierre had made it quite clear he didn't want to explain why he'd called at the house.

She looked down at the map, which she'd now spread over her lap. Pierre had drawn a ring around the restaurant they were heading for. It was over in the next valley, at the edge of a village she'd never heard of.

'We go straight over at the next crossroads and take a sharp right about two hundred metres after that.'

'Thanks.' He slowed down as the road narrowed and the bends became somewhat hazardous.

'Impossible to see what's coming towards you up here, with the thick hedgerows bushing out, but it's beautiful countryside, don't you think?' Pierre said, his voice much calmer now.

'It's fantastic up here on top of the hill. You can see for miles… Is that a wind farm over there on the next hill?'

'Yes. I don't think it spoils the view, do you? Some people were opposed to it.'

'I think it looks pretty with the white sails turning round in the wind,' Jacky said. 'Mmm… It's good to get away, isn't it? I might even be tempted to buy a car one day…if I stay here long enough. I came here in March to spend a month working alongside Debbie before she took maternity leave. I'm on a one-year contract so…'

'I'll be happy to take you for a drive whenever we're both free,' Pierre said, easily.

From the tone of his voice, Jacky deduced that the offer had been made entirely in the spirit of friendship. A favour to an old friend.

'Thanks, that would be nice…occasionally,' she said quietly, not wishing to sound too enthusiastic.

She glanced sideways to study Pierre's profile. The determined set of his jaw, the high cheekbones, the thick dark hair. She knew she'd love to come out here every day with him…just the two of them and no work to take up their attention. She checked her impossible thoughts, knowing that she would never be able to handle the emotional side if that were to happen.

As if sensing she was looking at him, he turned briefly and smiled. She coloured, thankful that he couldn't read her thoughts, but he was already looking back at the road.

'You look good with your hair streaming behind you,' he said softly. 'I know you took exception to the photographer commenting on your hair, but—'

'It depends who's making the comments,' she said quickly. 'I enjoy compliments from…well, from… friends.'

'I'm glad you count me as one of your friends.' He took one hand from the wheel and placed it momentarily over hers. She suppressed a shiver of sensual pleasure. She was sure Pierre had regarded it as a brotherly gesture but it had meant so much to her—much more than it should.

Both his hands were back on the steering-wheel now because they were driving down a steep narrow road. Suddenly Pierre had to slam on his brakes as a farmer, walking behind several cows, turned to put up his hand.

Pierre smiled. 'Can't very well overtake them, can we?'

'That's OK. According to the map, there's a farm just around the next corner. It's probably milking time so the farmer will be directing them into the farmyard soon.'

'I'm impressed with your navigation,' Pierre said, as the cows turned into a farmyard several metres down the road.

Jacky laughed. 'It's not difficult. My father taught me how to read a map after…after my mother left home. We used to go off on long journeys during the summer holidays and I was in charge of the navigation while Dad did the driving.'

'It must have been hard for you when your mother left you. I remember my mother saying something about it when I was away at medical school. How old were you?'

She swallowed hard as the memory of the confused feeling of being abandoned flooded back.

'I was ten… I'd had an idyllic carefree childhood until then. But I had to grow up quickly after that. It was impossibly hard for my father to cope with. I don't think he ever recovered.'

Pierre remained silent. He'd heard rumours about what had happened to the flamboyant Madame Shaftesbury, something about a lover in Paris, but he didn't want to upset Jacky by asking questions. She was a sensitive woman and he was sure that the air of bravado she was affecting now was all a façade. He'd heard that Jacky had been very close to her mother and being abandoned by her at such a young age had deeply affected her.

'My father did a great job of taking care of me,' Jacky said quietly. 'He was so happy when I decided to become a doctor and went off to medical school in London. He moved back to England and got a small flat nearby.'

'That must have been nice for both of you.'

'It was. I didn't want him to be left all alone in France. He was much older than my mother and he seemed to age a lot more after she left. I'd been worried about his general health for some time. Halfway through my first year at medical school he became ill and was diagnosed with bowel cancer. Apparently, the symptoms had been there for months but he'd done nothing about it. By the time he came into hospital it was too late to save him.'

She swallowed hard. 'At least I was able to be with him when…at the end.'

'I'm so sorry. You must have been devastated,' Pierre said gently, marvelling at the calm tone of Jacky's voice. But, then, she'd always been a tough girl. For a split second he thought of pulling over the car and taking her into his arms to comfort her. But he had the strangest feeling that he might be moved too deeply if he held that beautiful body against his. Again he reminded himself that Jacky might well misinterpret such a gesture. At all costs he must continue their easygoing friendliness.

Jacky looked out of her side of the car, holding back the tears. Pierre was now driving past the farmyard gate where the cows were now making their way to the milking shed. The peaceful rural scene reminded her so much of her childhood. Those halcyon days when she'd been part of a loving family, without a care in the world. At least she'd thought it had been a loving family. Both parents had loved her and her father had adored her mother. She had no idea if his love had been reciprocated by her mother.

'Daddy and I had no idea that Maman was going to leave us. She left a note for Daddy but he never told me what was in it, except that she wanted me to know she loved me. That made me think there was a chance she would come back, but…'

Jacky took a deep breath to steady her voice. 'But two days later the police arrived to tell us that Maman and her…her lover had met with an accident on the motorway. Apparently, they were driving down from Paris to his apartment in Cannes when their car crashed. They were both killed instantly.'

Pierre drew in his breath. 'I'm so sorry. My mother told me there had been a tragedy in your family but she wasn't sure what had happened.'

'Oh, the rumours flew round the village but nobody got

the story correct. Even I can only guess at some of the details.' She swallowed hard as the memories flooded back. 'It prepared me for some of the hard knocks I had to take later in life, I think.'

Pierre was slowing down as they came to the edge of a village. Red roofs on the cottages, neat flower-filled gardens.

'This is the place we're looking for. Marcel described the restaurant. It looks like that building over there…Chez Jules. That's the one!'

'Looks very swish!' Jacky said, in English.

Pierre laughed. 'Judging by the smart cars outside and Marcel's insistence that it was imperative to reserve a table, I think that's highly probable.'

It had obviously been a large, rather grand country house, *le manoir* of this pretty village. Once inside, Jacky was impressed by the decor. Parquet floors, high ceilings, antiques and objets d'art discreetly on display. The large ornate mirrors on the walls made the rooms seem bigger than they actually were.

A distinguished-looking man, black hair swept back from a high forehead to reveal greying temples, came forward to greet them and introduced himself as Jules, before offering them an aperitif at the cosy bar in the corner of the entrance hall.

Jacky chose a glass of kir, which was one of her favourite aperitifs, consisting of *crème de cassis* with white wine. Pierre had a glass of pastis. They chatted with the amiable Jules for a few minutes until their table was ready.

Going through to the dining room room, they found their table was set beside a window that looked over the garden. The waiter arrived with a large impressive menu.

Jacky chose *écrevisses* in a wine sauce while Pierre decided on *coquilles Saint-Jacques* as his starter.

'Mmm, those crayfish were delicious!' Jacky said a little later, finishing the last one before dipping her fingers in the lemon-scented finger bowl.

They had both chosen the wild duck with mushrooms which Jacky said was the most succulent duck she'd ever tasted. 'Sometimes I find duck can be dry but this was perfectly cooked.'

'It was excellent!' Pierre said, putting down his fork and smiling across the table at Jacky.

Jacky returned his smile. She'd noticed how their conversation throughout the meal had veered away from anything personal. They'd chatted about books they'd read, plays they'd seen, concerts they'd gone to and the merits of entertainment in Paris as opposed to London. It had been fun, stimulating, making her want to spend more time with Pierre, but she longed to find out more about his private life.

She looked down at the dessert menu which the waiter had just brought. *Tarte soufflé au chocolat* looked as if it would be delicious but she felt she couldn't eat another morsel.

'I'll just take coffee,' she told Pierre.

'*Moi aussi*. Shall we have our coffee out on the terrace?'

'That would be lovely. It's such a beautiful evening.'

The terrace had been built onto the back of the large house and looked out over the rose garden. The perfume of the flowers came wafting across on the evening breeze as they sat down on deeply cushioned wicker chairs. The sun had set behind the hills overlooking the village but the darkening sky was awash with crimson and gold ribbons and flecks.

'A perfect meal,' Jacky said, as she sipped her coffee. 'In a perfect setting.'

Pierre leaned back against the cushions of his chair. 'We didn't have anything approaching this superb restaurant in our little village, did we?'

'There was the café near the village shop.'

Pierre laughed. 'Hardly haute cuisine, was it?'

'True. But Papa and I used to spend a lot of time in there after Maman left home. Neither of us had learned how to cook so we used to go in at midday and make sure we had one good meal.'

Jacky sighed. '*Pauvre* Papa! My mother led him such a dance! Even as a young child, at the time when most children would think their life was normal, I knew Papa wasn't happy.'

'Why wasn't he happy?' Pierre asked gently.

Jacky sighed deeply. 'I often used to wonder how my parents got together in the first place. As I grew older they both, independently, explained how it came about. I realised it might have been because my middle-aged father felt suddenly young again when a youthful actress listened to what he was saying. When this charismatic young girl who, unlike the majority of his students at the university, actually showed an interest in his complicated theories about drama, whilst enjoying the compliments he showered on her about the way she'd performed or…'

She broke off, hesitating before continuing. She'd never discussed how she felt about her parents with anyone.

'Papa should never have married my mother,' she said. 'They were so different. The week before he died, as I was sitting at his bedside in hospital, he told me that he first met my mother when she was acting in a play at one of the small, relatively unknown theatres just outside London. He was an academic, a university lecturer, and he went backstage to discuss this contemporary, controversial play with the cast.'

Jacky leaned back against the chair as she remembered how flattered she'd been when her father had confided in her.

'Completely out of the blue, papa found himself falling in love with this vision of loveliness—that was how he described Maman to me—and before he could think twice, he'd invited her out for a drink. They talked about what was happening in contemporary theatre…never stopped talking, apparently, Papa told me! Well, she agreed to see him again. Shortly afterwards my father proposed and was amazed when my mother accepted.'

Pierre leaned forward. 'I remember that your mother was very beautiful.'

'But too young for my father! Maman once told me, after they'd had one of their rows, that she wished she'd stayed single. But she said that Papa had promised to take her back to France. That appealed to her because she was broke at the time and fed up with trying to earn a living in a small, not very successful group of actors. Escaping with my father to a new life had seemed so romantic!'

Jacky smiled as she remembered the day her mother had confided in her as if she had been a grown-up.

'Maman had thought it would be wonderful to live in a little village in Normandy. My father would write for a living instead of teaching at the university, and she would spend her days reading or going up to Paris to take an occasional interesting part on stage. She never ceased to hope that she might become a successful actress. But it never happened and I think she felt trapped and became disillusioned.'

'So that's how you came to be born in the village.'

Jacky nodded 'I think the romantic dream soon vanished when my parents found themselves struggling to make ends meet. Papa wrote a couple of textbooks, which were widely acclaimed in the academic press but didn't make much money. He tried his hand at fiction but that sank without trace.'

'I used to think what an interesting family you were.'

Jacky smiled. 'Interesting, but very poor. Unlike the wealthy Mellangers.'

'Oh, we weren't really wealthy! My grandfather had made some money from the château and vineyard he owned. My father chose to be a doctor but he inherited the château, all the land and the business. My grandfather stipulated everything was to be shared with me. My father was completely fair in this. We were very close. When my parents retired they chose to come out to Australia to be near me.'

'Are they still in Australia?'

'Yes, they have lots of friends so they stayed on when I returned to France. They'd bought a small house and invested the rest of the capital so that my share of Grandpapa's legacy would give me a private income. This was a great help when I was still a junior doctor. I was very lucky to have this financial security.'

Jacky smiled. 'Yes, you were. I remember standing outside the gates of your grandpapa's château and thinking how wonderful it must be to have such wealth.'

'Did you ever meet grandpapa?'

'*Une fois seulement.* Just the once.' Jacky took another sip of her coffee.

They were speaking French again because this was how they'd conversed all those years ago.

'I met your grandfather one day when my friend Sidonie and I decided to climb over the wall of the château into the orchard. We could see that there were some particularly succulent apples near the top of the wall on the other side, and Sidonie and I were hungry as usual. I got halfway over on the other side. I was facing the wall and planning to jump down backwards when dogs started barking and a pair of hands grabbed hold of my ankles and told me to stay still.'

'*Mon grandpapa?*'

Jacky grinned as she nodded. '*Oui.* I was terrified when this masterful voice started berating his dogs and telling them to be quiet. I was just a friend, your grandpapa told the dogs… A friend? I thought. I'm here to pinch your apples, *monsieur*!'

Pierre laughed. 'And what happened next?'

'Oh, your grandfather, having called off the dogs, lifted me down to safety and gave me a couple of beautiful apples, before escorting me to the gate.'

'Grandpapa was so kind. He was probably amused by the whole incident. And definitely relieved the dogs didn't harm you.' Pierre sighed. 'Yes, I was very lucky as a child, but…later on…' The tone of his voice changed. 'In adult life I've had some good luck and a lot of…'

'Unhappiness?' she said quietly.

He reached across the table and took hold of her hand. 'Yes, there has been a lot of unhappiness in my adult life. There have been some happy times as well but…'

He stood up and came round the table, drawing her to her feet. 'I don't want you to think I'm feeling sorry for myself,' he said. 'I think we shape our own destinies, don't you?'

She looked up into his eyes and thought she could see a hint of vulnerability behind the strong expression. 'But there are so many things over which we have no control,' she whispered, suddenly feeling as if they were the only people in the restaurant.

Here on the terrace outside the dining room, they were quite alone, but nearby the late diners were still lingering inside. But she didn't care if anyone came out and saw them standing in this wonderful embrace, their arms lightly touching as they each listened to what the other had to say.

The world didn't exist any more except for this tiny corner where she was with the most wonderful man she'd ever known. It was as if Pierre was her hero, come to claim her after all these years…the stuff of fairy-tales but a totally fictitious, impossible dream!

For a brief instant she knew how her father had felt when he'd connected with her mother for the first time. It didn't make sense…but, then, falling in love never did. It was totally irrational…out of this world…and try as she could, she was finding it impossible to fight against her true feelings.

'Oh, yes, we do shape our own destinies,' she whispered.

Pierre lowered his head and kissed her, his lips as light as a butterfly's wing. She suppressed the ecstatic moan that threatened to betray how emotionally and hopelessly involved she was.

'Monsieur le docteur?'

The waiter had come out onto the terrace. *'Je m'excuse mais Monsieur Jules demande s'il peut vous offrir un petit digestif avec le café.'*

Pierre dropped his arms to his side as he politely declined the offer of a liqueur with their coffee.

Jacky sat down in her chair, breathing heavily. The moment had passed. She'd been saved from making a complete fool of herself. She could hear Pierre asking for the bill.

The magic of that moment wasn't rekindled during the

drive back to St Martin sur mer. Pierre seemed to be at pains to return to the polite friendly tone they'd adopted from the beginning of their evening out together. He asked for directions to her apartment, stopped outside, climbed out to open the passenger door and stood on the pavement, looking down at her with an enigmatic expression.

She looked up at him, searching his eyes for any hint that the magic might return. But, no, he was simply the good friend from the past. The big brother she wished she'd had. She could ask him in for a drink, but she didn't think that was a good idea. She couldn't bear the thought that her offer might be turned down.

'It was a lovely evening, Pierre,' she said, affecting her brave 'you don't have to worry about me, I'm not going to drag you inside' smile.

He took her face in his hands and kissed her gently on the lips. As he raised his head he looked down at her, his eyes once more vibrant and expectant.

Jacky turned away and walked with a purposeful stride to her door.

CHAPTER THREE

As PIERRE drove away from Jacky's apartment he felt a deep sense of frustration. He glanced in his rear-view mirror to see if Jacky had gone inside. Yes, there was no sign of her. She'd made it quite clear that she didn't intend to linger and prolong their evening together.

He pressed his foot down on the accelerator. He'd played it very badly tonight, coming on so strong when they'd been having their coffee. He hadn't been able to help himself but he mustn't allow himself to become so emotionally involved with Jacky again.

His frustration, both emotional and physical, was increasing. He groaned. Maybe he should stop seeing her altogether in off-duty situations. The trouble was, he found her so attractive. The pretty, vivacious, wild child had grown into the most beautiful, sexy, intelligent, interesting woman he'd ever met.

And that was the problem he'd avoided since he'd lost Liliane. When Liliane had died in childbirth, bearing the child he'd longed for, he'd vowed to stay true to her for the rest of his life. The sense of guilt he'd felt at her funeral in Paris had been almost more than he'd been able to bear. He'd learned to live with it but there was no way he could ever forget.

He sighed as he took one hand off the steering-wheel to adjust his rear-view mirror. The car behind was coming up too close and this was a speed-restricted area. The car passed and he swore under his breath. There were always idiots like that driving too fast, causing accidents and more work for the Urgences department.

He gripped the wheel as his thoughts returned to Liliane. His wife hadn't been sure if she would make a good mother but he'd told her he'd always wanted a family. He'd said he was sure she would enjoy family life. And the poor girl had paid with her life…the ultimate sacrifice. She'd given him his much-wanted son. The anguish of knowing about her self-sacrifice was always with him…the guilt…

He pulled into his drive. He switched off the engine and sat with his hands still clutching the wheel, his head bowed over it as he reviewed the situation. For five years he'd stayed true to Liliane. For the first year he'd lived like a monk…a monk with the responsibility of looking after his son.

He closed his eyes as the memories flooded back. He remembered the day when he'd decided that he couldn't go on denying his physical needs any longer. He'd decided he should start dating again, physically enjoying his time with another woman but mentally remaining true to Liliane.

He'd made a point of only dating women who couldn't possibly become important in his life. And he'd enjoyed a few short, interesting affairs with like-minded partners who'd also only wanted a temporary relationship.

The problem had been when he'd dated Simone for a few months and had taken her home on several occasions. She'd been a warm-hearted person who loved children, and Christophe had begun to regard her as some kind of mother figure. When the relationship had ended, Christophe had been devastated. So he'd had to make a rule for himself that he wouldn't introduce his girlfriends to his son. The easiest way around this was not to talk about his son in the first place. Which also meant he couldn't entertain his girlfriends at home.

But Jacky was different! He'd wanted to share all his secrets with her tonight. He'd longed to open up and confide everything. But that would have led to impossible emotional problems. Opening up, sharing confidences with someone like Jacky meant emotional involvement…something he'd avoided since Liliane had died. Even now, he was having trouble damping down the real emotion that he'd felt during the evening.

He raised his head from the steering-wheel, suddenly aware that someone was standing beside the car.

'*Ça va, Pierre?*'

Nadine was looking down at him with a concerned expression.

'I heard the sound of your car and when you didn't come inside I—'

'It's OK. I'm fine, Nadine. I'll come inside in a moment. But you must go to bed now. Is Christophe all right?'

'Yes, he settled down well after he'd seen you this evening.'

'I thought he would. Goodnight, Nadine.'

'Goodnight, Pierre.'

Pierre watched his son's nanny return inside, leaving the door open for him to follow her. As he pressed the switch that brought the roof of his car down he felt relieved that Nadine seemed to be settled in the job at last. It was early days. He'd been employing her now for three months and she'd agreed to leave Paris and transfer to St Martin sur mer. She was a good, conscientious, intelligent girl and he hoped she would stay because Christophe seemed to like her.

That was another problem. None of the nannies he'd

employed had stayed as long as he would have wished. He'd given them very generous salaries, but they'd invariably decided to move on. Christophe wasn't the easiest child to cope with. Now that he was going to the *école primaire* in St Martin during the day, it meant that Nadine could have more free time. Unlike the previous nannies who'd invariably become tired of the long hours they'd been in charge.

He got out of the car. As he walked to the door he knew it was only a matter of time before Nadine decided to go back to Paris. She'd already indicated that she wanted to spend more time in Paris with her boyfriend. When he'd first employed her, the fact that she'd had a steady boyfriend had been a plus. There had been no chance of her trying to flirt with him, as had happened with two of the women who'd worked for him previously.

He had the awful feeling that soon he would be looking for a new nanny and he would have to give Christophe as much tender loving care as he could during the transition period.

He took the stairs two at a time, anxious to see his son. He felt guilty that he'd been out this evening after working all day. He should have spent quality time with Christophe, but he'd make it up to him tomorrow. It was essential that he continue with his career, and leisure time was equally important if he was to prevent himself becoming obsessed with his family problems.

Christophe's bedroom was next to his own. Nadine, whose bedroom was at the other end of the landing, had left Christophe's door open so that she could hear him if he called out. Pierre went into the room and sat down on the chair at the side of his son's bed. The soft fair hair was fanned out over the pillow. Christophe was sucking his thumb.

Pierre smiled as he gently removed the thumb from his son's mouth. It gave him such comfort and that was something his precious boy needed. If only he'd had a mother with him from birth…a constant figure, always there for him…he would have felt more secure and wouldn't display the tantrums that the nannies found so difficult to cope with.

Pierre bent his head and kissed the soft velvet of his son's cheek. Christophe stirred in his sleep, opened his eyes and reached up to put his arms around Pierre's neck.

'*Papa, je t'aime,*' he whispered, before closing his eyes and falling back into a deep sleep.

Pierre swallowed the lump in his throat. 'I love you, too, Christophe,' he whispered as he pulled the sheet up around his son's shoulders.

He went quietly into his own room. Closing the door, he leaned against it for a moment, looking across his moonlit bedroom. The windows were still wide open, allowing the scent of the flowers with a hint of the salty breeze from the sea to waft across the room. It would have been the perfect setting for a romantic liaison with Jacky tonight if only he'd dared to invite her back here. But a fling would be impossible with someone like Jacky. He knew instinctively that it would mean too much to him…and he couldn't become disloyal when he'd promised himself he would stay faithful for ever.

He groaned out loud. If only he were a carefree bachelor, someone without ties or responsibilities! Someone who didn't bear a permanent sense of obligation and guilt towards the woman who'd sacrificed her life to bear him a son…

Jacky ran up the stairs to her first-floor apartment. She didn't want to hang about down there—it would give

Pierre completely the wrong idea. He'd made it clear he wasn't interested in her in a romantic way. Which was exactly as it should be because she didn't want any romantic complications in her life ever again.

She let herself into the apartment, closed the door, slipped off her sandals and went through to the bedroom. Sinking down on the bed, she rubbed the soles of her bare feet. All that walking around at the hospital today had taken its toll. She lay back on the bed, propping herself up on the pillows.

Her thoughts turned to Pierre, the strong, handsome, athletic young man she'd admired as a child and the new version of older, still devastatingly handsome, grieving widower. She felt glad that she'd managed to make him smile a lot this evening. The little-boy-lost expression had soon disappeared when they'd started swapping stories from the past. One thing they hadn't done was discuss their previous relationships. She knew nothing about the beautiful wife who'd died and Pierre was no wiser about Paul.

She sighed as she thought about her ex husband. She remembered how she'd loved him so much at the beginning of their marriage that she'd cherished every moment they'd been together. They had been fellow medical students, both hard up but happy to be in love. During their final year, Paul had moved into her flat. They'd been young and naïve and it had been great to have their own little love nest. Paul had proposed. The idea of getting married seemed so romantic, he'd told her... As had the idea of starting a family.

The family idea had been Paul's initially. He'd said it wouldn't make any difference. She could take time out and then continue with her career. He'd help all he could during the pregnancy and afterwards. And she'd totally believed he meant it! Actually, with the benefit of hindsight, he probably had meant it at the time. It had just been another of his hare-brained schemes as far as he was concerned! Love and fidelity hadn't come into the equation.

How could she have been so wrong in her character assessment of him? Why hadn't she realised that he was incapable of staying faithful to anyone? As soon as the reality of her pregnancy had begun to lose its appeal, she'd sensed that Paul had become restless, spending more and more time away from the flat. But still she hadn't suspected the worst-case scenario…that he would leave her.

She would never be able to forget how he'd walked out on her when she'd been six months pregnant. He'd found someone else, he'd told her—one of the nurses he'd been working with in Orthopaedics—and this time he thought he could make the relationship last. Paul and his new partner had changed hospitals to escape the scandal surrounding the marriage break-up and the outrage of his colleagues on learning that he'd abandoned his pregnant wife.

Basically, Paul had never grown up and he'd worked hard at his Peter Pan image. Looking back, Jacky decided that the reality of fatherhood, with all its responsibility, had suddenly frightened him. The hospital staff who'd cared for her during her traumatic labour had sent a message to Paul. He'd arrived the day after their baby had died.

She remembered how he'd stood awkwardly by her bedside for a few minutes while she'd lain still, traumatised by the whole awful experience of the painful, precipitous birth when she'd nearly lost her life. She had been relieved when a nurse had asked him to leave so that she could be heavily sedated again. She'd closed her eyes and drifted off into the oblivion that had been her only relief from the suffering and trauma of losing her precious baby.

She put her hands over her abdomen, in her mind reliving some of the agony she'd endured. But this wouldn't happen again. She remembered the obstetrician who'd cared for her and how sympathetic his eyes had been when he'd finally told her the truth. It had been something of a comfort to her that he was a personal friend and colleague.

On the day when she had finally been allowed to leave hospital he'd told her that, because of the damage to her internal organs, her chances of conceiving another child were extremely remote. Extensive surgery at a future date might improve her chances if she wished to go through with a further pregnancy, but she should be prepared for a similar experience of childbirth in the unlikely event that she should conceive.

She'd told him there wouldn't be a next time.

She grabbed a tissue from the box and blew her nose. No point getting morbid about it. She tried to banish the memories that often came to her in her sleep as nightmares but the clear images refused to disappear. She was once again working in Accident and Emergency, eight months pregnant. Still working because she didn't want to have time to think about Paul, about what the future held now that she was going to be a single mother. And she needed to make it clear to her medical colleagues that she was a career doctor who took her work seriously.

She wasn't going to give up working after the baby was born. Oh, no! She was going to arrange excellent childcare even if, initially, it took most of her salary. She'd actually been making enquiries about childcare at an agency in London during her lunchtime break the day that Simon was born, she remembered.

She'd been to the agency and hurried back to work. Her first patient had been a drunk who'd been fighting in a pub but appeared to have passed out. As she'd bent over to begin suturing a wound on his face, caused by a broken bottle, he'd lashed out with his fist and hit her in the abdomen. Remembering the agonising pain now, her fingers tightened over her abdomen as if to reassure herself that she wasn't hurt...that she wasn't going to feel the hot, sticky blood trickling down between her legs and...

She turned on her side and buried her face in the pillow. She'd survived...but only just! Thanks to expert medical attention from her colleagues. She'd even been strong enough to hold her much-wanted but fatally injured baby in her arms...until his little chest had stopped moving up and down and she'd had to accept that...that she was alone again.

She sat up and grabbed another tissue. She'd never given in to self-pity and she wasn't going to now. She stripped off, pulled on her robe and padded barefoot over to the bathroom. A long soak in the bath would relax her and then she would sleep. Because if she simply closed her eyes now there would be too many unpleasant memories crowding into her dreams...

Jacky found that the days at the hospital were always busy in Urgences. But that was why she'd chosen to work in Accident and Emergency in the first place. She never knew what each day would bring. And working with Pierre was always stimulating. He exuded confidence and a vibrant determination to succeed in whatever he was doing.

Two weeks on from the day when they'd resuscitated

Dominic, the little toddler who'd almost died, they were both standing at the main entrance to Urgences, saying goodbye to him. As Jacky looked down at the tiny, now perfectly fit child she remembered how determined Pierre had been on that awful day when his life had hung in the balance.

The grateful parents had insisted that Pierre and Jacky be photographed with their little son before they left.

'Dominic! Regarde papa!' The boy's smiling mother was directing her son's attention towards the camera, but Dominic wanted to look everywhere but where he was supposed to.

He was busily chattering to Pierre now, asking him if he was coming home with him today. After Pierre had told the little boy he had to stay at the hospital to work, he directed Dominic's attention to the camera. This time it worked and Dominic gave a big happy smile for his father.

Jacky sighed as they went back inside. 'It's good to see Dominic looking so fit but I've grown fond of him during the last two weeks. I shall miss our little chats together.'

'You love children, don't you?' Pierre said quietly.

He stopped walking and put his hand on her arm. He'd recognised that children were very important to Jacky as he'd watched her working during the last couple of weeks. An admirable trait, but that was one of the reasons he'd held back from asking her out again. During the course of conversation he would find it hard not to tell her about his son, Christophe. She would want to see him, and Christophe would like her a lot—well, who wouldn't? And he didn't want his son to be upset when Jacky stopped seeing him.

'Let's go and have a coffee while the department is quiet,' he said. He enjoyed working with her and the few minutes they occasionally snatched together in the medical staff café had become precious to him.

'I've got a cafetière in my office,' Jacky said, as they walked on down the corridor. 'The coffee I make is much better than the coffee in the café. I took over Debbie's office when she went on maternity leave. We shared it for the first month I was here when we were working together. Between us we turned it into a room with some of the home comforts that busy doctors need during the times they can take a break.'

Pierre smiled. 'I was wondering when you'd invite me in. It's definitely by invitation only, isn't it?'

Jacky pushed open the door of her office. 'Of course.'

Pierre looked around. 'It's definitely cosy,' he said, grinning as he reverted to English again. He found he enjoyed brushing up his English with Jacky.

Jacky laughed. 'That's estate-agent speak for small, isn't it?'

'Absolutely! But you've managed to cram in some comfy chairs, which is what's needed.'

He sank down into one, spreading his long legs in front of him while Jacky filled the kettle at the small sink in the corner of the room. She stepped over Pierre's long legs, which seemed to take up half the room, and perched on the side of her desk as she waited for the kettle to boil.

'Yes, it was good to see little Dominic looking so happy,' Pierre commented. 'The outcome could have been very different.'

Jacky nodded. 'I've been in to see him almost every day.'

'I've noticed you're particularly fond of caring for our small patients. Didn't you want to have children of your own when you were married, Jacky?'

She got up from the desk and went back to spoon coffee

into the cafetière, concentrating on the task so that she wouldn't have to look at Pierre. She took a deep breath to ease the tension as she spoke, keeping her voice as steady as she could.

'I did have a baby...for a short time...but he died...' She swallowed hard. 'How do you like your coffee, strong, weak or...?' Her voice choked.

Pierre had risen up and moved swiftly to put his arms around her. 'I'm sorry,' he said. 'I had no idea that...'

She looked up into his eyes, which held such a tender, comforting expression that she wanted to remain in his arms for a long time, gathering some of the strength that seemed to flow from his strong muscular body. She felt that if she could stand here with Pierre's arms still around her, the hurt would ease for a while.

Pierre could feel the trembling of her lovely, delicately formed, curvaceous frame as he held her close to him. He could tell that she was putting her trust in him, just as she had done when she'd been a child. But this time there was real sensual emotion flowing between them. His initial reaction had been to comfort her but now his feelings were of a different kind.

Slowly he bent his head and kissed her gently on her cheek. He felt genuine surprise as she turned her head towards him, her lips parted in anticipation. As his lips closed on hers he felt her body relaxing against his. She'd stopped trembling and her lovely curves slotted against his muscles in all the right places. For a few seconds he allowed himself to be roused by her nearness before pulling himself away.

Jackie moved swiftly away as she tried to return to reality. Pierre sat down in the chair and took a deep breath to calm himself. As he'd initially suspected, becoming involved with Jacky would mean a total involvement of his emotions. Something he'd promised himself he could never do again. Besides which, he wasn't sure that Jackie, in the vulnerable state she was in, would be ready to leave the past behind her and move on either.

How the poor girl must have suffered! He could hardly bear to think about the trauma of losing a child. The thought of life without his precious Christophe was unimaginable.

'I'm feeling OK again,' Jacky said, as she poured the boiling water over the coffee grounds in the cafetière. 'I always get upset when I have to think or talk about my little Simon.'

Pierre collected a couple of cups and poured out the coffee, setting the cups down on the small coffee-table. They pulled up their chairs and sat looking at each other, a palpable feeling of rapport between them.

'How old was Simon when…?'

'Just over two hours.'

Pierre drew in his breath. What could he say? No wonder Jacky often wore that sad, vulnerable expression. But he'd noticed that if ever he looked at her when she was in a pensive, contemplative mood, she immediately put on her act-of-bravado face. She was the sort of woman who didn't want pity. Comfort possibly? But not pity.

'I feel very privileged that you've taken me into your confidence,' he said gently. She decided to go for it. He seemed so approachable now. 'Pierre, the small child I heard when I waited in the car outside your house. Is the child yours?'

Pierre hesitated. 'Yes, that's my five-year-old son, Christophe.'

'Why haven't you spoken about him?'

He turned away. 'It's because… Actually, I'll explain

it all another time. I have my reasons, which are a bit complicated.'

'There isn't a problem with your son...healthwise, I mean, is there?' she said, trying to be as tactful as she possibly could.

Pierre turned back to face her. 'Christophe is extremely fit and active,' he said evenly.

He paused. It would have to happen. He couldn't treat Jacky in the way he'd treated the unimportant women who'd briefly been part of his life. 'Perhaps you could come and meet him some time.'

There! He'd taken an irrevocable step. How he was going to cope with the consequences of introducing someone Christophe couldn't fail to bond with he had no idea! He wasn't going to look too far into the future. He wanted to see more of Jacky. Much more than a few minutes during a break from work at the hospital! And for that there would be a price to pay. Nothing worthwhile was ever easy.

His pager was bleeping. Jacky handed him the phone from her desk. '*Tout de suite!*' he replied after listening for a few seconds.

'Another problem at sea. A couple of casualties arriving.'

Jacky set her cup down on the sink and followed Pierre out into the corridor. Together they hurried down to the main reception area. Marie showed Jacky into the treatment room where the two injured men were lying on examination couches.

A paramedic briefed them before leaving. It appeared that one patient, a waterski instructor, had been driving the boat which had been towing the other man on waterskis. When the man on the skis had attempted to ski on one leg, a recognised manoeuvre during the waterski course of lessons, his foot had become entangled in his ski. As he'd tried to shake off the ski, the weight of the water had pulled the ski down, and his leg had been wrenched sideways, causing him painful injuries as he'd fallen into the water.

The instructor had switched off his engine and scrambled over the back of the boat to rescue his pupil. But in doing so he'd overstretched one leg and was in intense pain himself.

Jacky began to examine the pupil, who was an Englishman on holiday, while Pierre concentrated on the instructor, a Frenchman who worked at the local watersports school.

Jacky took a brief case history from her patient. Jeff Harris, age 27, from London. Physically fit before this accident.

'I'm glad you're English, Doctor,' Jeff said. 'My French isn't so good. I probably misunderstood what Franck instructed me to do. He told me to release the ski when he signalled and ski on one leg, but I hadn't realised how hard it would be. We'd practised it on dry land but—'

He broke off and grimaced. 'My thigh is so painful...the one that got twisted round, and— Ooh...'

'Let's take a look, shall we?' Jacky put her fingers gently over the rapidly bruising area. 'I'm going to give you a painkilling injection so I can examine this area more carefully.'

Jeff closed his eyes and clenched his teeth. 'Thanks, Doc.'

Further examination when her patient had been partially sedated revealed that when Jeff's leg had been wrenched sideways there had been severe damage to the ligaments.

She asked Pierre to join her for a moment to confirm her diagnosis.

'It looks as if the ilio-femoral ligament has been torn away from the bone,' she told Pierre.

After examination he agreed with her diagnosis. 'Better get an X-ray to check on the state of the femur. Franck, my patient, has torn his Achilles tendon. I need to consult with the orthopaedic firm to see if they can operate today. While your patient's in X-Ray, would you check on mine, please?'

As soon as she was able, Jacky moved across the treatment room to be with Franck. He looked considerably older than Jeff as he turned his head to look up at her.

'Couldn't have happened at a worse time, Doctor,' he told her in French. 'We're at the height of the season and now I'll be laid up for weeks apparently.'

'Well, you'll be able to get around once you've had the operation and you've got a cast on your leg, but energetic manoeuvres won't be possible.'

Franck groaned. 'I knew I'd done something serious when I climbed out of my seat on the boat. It felt as if somebody had shot me in the back of the leg.' He hesitated. 'Do you think I could have a sip of water?'

'I'm sorry, Franck, there's a possibility you may be going to Theatre soon if Pierre can arrange it. Ah, here he is now. Franck was asking if—'

'They can operate in an hour,' Pierre said, going over to his patient to explain what was to happen.

Jeff was being wheeled in again from X-Ray. Jacky checked the X-rays, using the light box on the wall. As she had thought, there was no damage to the bone but considerable damage to the ilio-femoral ligament.

'I'm going to splint your thigh and pack ice around it to reduce the swelling,' she told Jeff. 'After that you'll be taken on to the preliminary orthopaedic unit for further treatment.'

Jeff nodded, wearily. 'Thanks, Doctor. Can you come with me to act as my interpreter?'

Jacky smiled. 'I'll come and see you settled in but then I'll have to get back here to Accident and Emergency. Some of the staff do speak a bit of English. If you find you have a real problem you can get a message to me. Just say, *"Je voudrais parler à Docteur Jacky Manson."*'

Jeff grinned. 'That means I'd like to speak to you, doesn't it? I remember that much from my schooldays.'

By the end of the day, Jacky had seen a great many patients but she found time to call in to see Jeff. He was propped up in bed, watching the small television suspended on the wall at the end of his bed. He pulled off his headphones when he saw Jacky arriving.

'How're you feeling now?'

'I'd like some more painkillers, but I don't know how to ask. I'm watching this stuff on TV that I don't understand just to take my mind off the pain.'

'Yes, there's no need to suffer any more than you have to.' Jacky glanced at the notes and saw that her stipulation about four-hourly medication hadn't been adhered to. She'd have a word with Sister on her way out. And she'd make sure that Sister found an English-speaking member of staff if there were any problems with Jeff.

Walking back down the corridor, after she'd organised the painkillers for Jeff, she met Pierre.

'I'm just going to check on Franck,' Pierre said. 'The orthopaedic firm have operated and told me that as far as they can tell at this stage his repair of the Achilles tendon has been successful. He'll need to keep the cast on for several weeks, of course.'

He pulled a wry grin. 'I'm going to tell Franck it would have been much quicker to break a bone than snap his Achilles tendon.'

Jacky smiled. 'Do you think he'll appreciate that?'

Pierre smiled back. 'Oh, Franck's got a good sense of humour. I met him on the beach last week when I went to his watersports business to ask about hiring a boat. I thought I might take Christophe with me one day.'

'Would Christophe enjoy that, do you think?'

'I'm sure he would.' He hesitated. 'If you're free this evening, come round for supper and you can meet him.'

'I'd love to!' She hadn't meant to sound so eager! But the invitation had taken her completely by surprise.

Pierre hadn't really expected her to accept so quickly. But he told himself the die was now cast. He couldn't back out.

'Come round to the house as soon as you're free. Nadine, Christophe's nanny, will be there with him if I'm held up here. *À tout à l'heure*, Jacky.'

'Yes, see you later.'

She drew in her breath as she walked on in the opposite direction. She had the distinct feeling that Pierre's invitation had been made on the spur of the moment and he was already regretting it, otherwise why had he made a point of keeping her outside when she'd been there a couple of weeks ago?

And she'd been so unsophisticated just now, jumping at the chance to go round to his house! Perhaps she should pretend she'd remembered a previous engagement.

She turned round but Pierre had already disappeared along the corridor. Oh, well, she would go along tonight and see what all the mystery was about. If she felt the least bit unwelcome, she would make an excuse and go back to her apartment.

As she walked along to the staff cloakroom she remembered the feel of Pierre's strong arms around her that morning. Maybe it would be worth running the gauntlet of a few unwelcoming vibes just to spend a whole evening with him.

CHAPTER FOUR

JACKY looked up at the imposing façade of Pierre's house. She was glad that Pierre had explained about Grandpapa Mellanger's legacy. It needed a lot of inherited money to buy a place like this! The old man must have really loved his grandson to make such good provision for him.

She remembered seeing the two of them together in the village once—shortly after she'd been apprehended climbing over the Mellanger wall. The old man and his grandson had appeared to have a very close relationship. She hadn't been surprised when Pierre had told her that his grandfather had stipulated in his will that Pierre should receive his full share of the legacy while his parents were still alive.

Looking up now at the front of the house, she admired the ivy-clad stone walls. They were punctuated by large casement windows thrown open to allow glimpses of the intriguing interior, which gave the place an inviting ambience. Someone looking in from outside—as she was unashamedly doing now!—couldn't quite see what was going on in there but got the feeling it was a real family house.

During the walk here from her apartment she'd been barely able to contain her excitement! She felt like a child who'd finally been invited to a party at a house which had been previously inaccessible to her.

She told herself to grow up and stop fantasising! She walked the last few metres up the drive and paused in front of the sturdy oak door. Somebody had recently rubbed the huge brass knocker so that it shone in the evening sunlight. No car in the front drive, she noticed. There was a small car, probably belonging to the nanny, parked at the side by a door that looked as if it led into the kitchen.

She'd rather hoped that Pierre would be here by now. He was later than she'd expected. She didn't want to appear too eager. She should have had the panache to arrive fashionably late. It might be an idea to backtrack and wait at the end of the road for a while until... Now, that definitely was a childish idea! No, she would brazen it out.

Why was it that she was feeling so much like the youngster she'd been way back in the village when Pierre had been a tall, exciting boy she'd desperately wanted to get to know. She raised her hand towards the door knocker but didn't quite reach it before the door swung open as if by magic.

'*Bonsoir, Dr Manson. Entrez, s'il vous plaît.*'

The girl ushering her through must be Nadine. She was friendly, but had an air of agitation about her, as if she'd been interrupted in the middle of doing something important.

'*Dr Mellanger est toujours à l'hôpital, madame,*' the girl said as Jacky stepped into the high-ceilinged entrance hall. 'I hope you do not mind waiting.'

Jacky followed Nadine along a polished parquet-floored corridor to a long terrace at the back of the house. A small, fair-haired boy was sitting at a table, drawing a picture with some thick crayons. He glanced briefly at her but returned to his drawing without uttering a word or making eye contact. Jacky's heart went out to him.

For a fleeting moment she thought of her own son, little Simon, who would have been old enough to draw pictures with crayons now. She would have been admiring his pictures, leaning over him to give encouragement. They would have gone through the toddler years together and…

Quickly, she stemmed her impossible longing for what might have been as she moved towards Christophe. But before she could reach him, his nanny put her hand on Jacky's arm and took her to one side.

'Please, Dr Manson, I need your help,' she whispered, in an urgent tone. 'You are here for the evening, yes?'

'Yes, that's correct. What's the problem?'

'I have just received a message from a hospital ten miles away from here. My boyfriend was driving from Paris to meet me this evening. He has been involved in an accident and has been taken to hospital. The nurse who phoned said he is asking to see me. Would you take care of Christophe so that I can drive over there now?'

Jacky was immediately full of concern for the poor girl. 'Is your boyfriend badly hurt?' she asked in a sympathetic tone.

'I don't know. I was told his life is not in danger but he will have to stay in hospital at least for tonight. Please! Dr Mellanger is often very late when an emergency delays him at the hospital.'

Jacky wanted to help Christophe's nanny if she could, but she felt she should have a quick word with Pierre first. 'I'll phone Dr Mellanger and see how long he's going to be before he gets home.'

'But I have to go now!'

Jacky heard the anxiety in the girl's voice. She reasoned that if her boyfriend's life wasn't in danger, a few minutes wouldn't make much difference. But the poor girl was working herself up into a state of extreme distress. Young Christophe had climbed down from his chair and was coming over to see what all the fuss was about. She didn't want the boy to become as agitated as his nanny. Children picked up emotional vibes very easily.

'All right, Nadine, I'll explain to Pierre. But you will call from the hospital and let Dr Mellanger know when you'll be back, won't you?'

'*Bien sûr, merci, merci… Au revoir…*'

'Nadine!' the little boy cried as his nanny hurried out through the door. 'Nadine!'

'*Au revoir*, Christophe!' the girl called as she slammed the kitchen door at the side of the house. Seconds later Jacky heard the sound of a car engine starting up.

The little boy stamped his foot and started screaming.

Jacky knelt down and put her arms around the trembling little body. At first he resisted but as she spoke soothingly to him in French he calmed down and stopped screaming. When she relaxed her grip the small child stared up at her.

'Who are you?' he asked, his little face puzzled and anxious. 'Are you a friend of Papa?'

His French words still held the charming Parisian accent which she loved to hear when Pierre spoke to her. He was uncannily like his father. The expressive eyes, the high cheekbones in the otherwise baby face. His blond flyaway hair was already turning dark in places. He would be even more like Pierre when the baby hair gave way to a darker shade of brown.

She'd been alarmed by Christophe's violent reaction to Nadine's departure but it hadn't surprised her. Having been left with a total stranger, the little boy was confused about what was happening.

Gently she explained to Christophe who she was, little by little trying to gain his confidence. As he listened she felt she was getting somewhere with him. She moved to-

wards one of the wicker armchairs on the terrace and held
out her arms towards him.

'Would you like me to tell you a story?'

The five-year-old hesitated. His face puckered as if he
was going to cry.

'I'll tell you about Cendrillon,' she said quietly. 'Have
you heard that story?'

Christophe nodded before shyly moving towards her,
climbing easily onto her lap.

'Would you like to hear the story of Cinderella?' she
asked again.

Christophe smiled up at her. *'Oui, madame.'*

'Je m'appelle Jacky.'

'Jacky.' The little boy tried out the unfamiliar name as
he settled himself on her lap to listen to the story.

'Il y avait une fois…' Jacky remembered how her
mother had always started the story of Cinderella with
those words. She remembered Cinderella had always been
one of her favourites and her mother had told it to her so
beautifully when she'd been small.

Her mother's voice had been so expressive. All her
pent-up, frustrated acting talents had come out in the ren-
dition. Once she'd stopped her mother in the middle of
the story and asked if they could dress up and act the
story together, and her mother had readily agreed. It had
been such fun! Maman had been Cinderella, she remembered, and she'd had to play the parts of both the ugly
sisters!

She came back to the present and looked down at the
little boy on her lap. Tonight, with Pierre's small son,
Jacky was simply trying to gain his confidence and keep
him happy.

He laid his head against her shoulder as he listened.
Without pausing in her story, she glanced at her watch.

What was keeping Pierre? Why hadn't he phoned to say that he would be late? What would he say when she told him that Nadine—?

Her mobile began to ring. It was almost as if she'd sent Pierre a telepathic message.

'Jacky, I'll come and pick you up on my way back from the hospital.'

He sounded weary.

'I'm already here—I mean at your house—and—'

'Oh, I'm sorry you arrived first. There were several emergency admissions just as I was leaving…one of them a man with chest pains. The cardiac team were already involved with another emergency. I admitted him to Intensive Care and worked on him with the night staff who'd only just arrived. We've got him stabilised and the cardiac team have taken over.'

He paused as if to catch his breath. 'I hope Nadine is looking after you.'

'Actually…actually she had to go off and see her boy-friend who's been involved in a car accident. He's in a hospital about ten miles away. She went off in her car and—'

'Poor Nadine. Is he badly injured?'

'She was told his life isn't in danger.'

'Thank goodness for that. So she'll be coming back tonight?' he said hopefully, as he quickly reviewed his commitments for the next day.

Jacky could tell he was frowning at the unexpected news.

'I've asked her to phone from the hospital,' Jacky said.

'*C'est Papa?*' Christophe asked, reaching for Jacky's phone.

She smiled. '*Oui, c'est Papa, mais—*'

'*Papa!*' the little boy said happily as Jacky relinquished her phone. '*Où es tu?*'

'I'm at the hospital. Just coming home, Christophe.'

'Jacky's telling me the story about Cinderella. Come home quickly so you can hear the bit where she changes into a pumpkin…or something like that. I've forgotten what happens but Jacky will tell me.'

Jacky heard Pierre laughing over the phone.

''*À bientôt, Papa!*' Christophe said, smiling as he snuggled back against Jacky.

Pierre settled himself into the driving seat and started the engine. Half of him was feeling happy that Christophe was enjoying Jacky's company and the other half, the sensible half, was reminding him that this was exactly what he hadn't wanted to happen. If only he'd got home first, he could have introduced Jacky to Christophe and then asked Nadine to put him to bed.

On second thoughts, that would have been a churlish thing to do, he told himself as he drove out through the wide entrance to the hospital, pausing to acknowledge the wave of the porter on duty. Christophe was obviously enjoying himself with Jacky. And Jacky—he knew how she loved children—would probably be enjoying having his son all to herself. He hoped she wasn't finding his son to be too poignant a reminder of what she'd lost when her own baby son had died.

He sighed as he turned into the main road. How was he going to cope when his relationship with Jacky reached the point where he had to hold back? As it would. Because, with the strong feelings he had for her already, he knew he was in danger of falling in love…something that simply mustn't happen.

He pushed his emotional problems to the back of his

mind as he remembered the practicalities of the evening ahead. He'd invited Jacky for supper. Better get something from the delicatessen. He drove right round the roundabout and headed back towards the main street of St Martin. Jacques, the owner of the delicatessen, was just closing up as Pierre screeched to a halt in front of the shop.

Pierre leapt over the door of his car without opening it. *'S'il vous plaît, Jacques…'*

The portly middle-aged man smiled at his late customer. *'Pour vous, Dr Mellanger, le magasin est ouvert pour cinq minutes encore.'*

'Five minutes is all I need,' Pierre said, as he followed the kindly owner back into his shop. *'Merci beaucoup.'*

Jacques began to show Pierre everything he'd put back in the fridge or the cold store.

Pierre pointed at a succulent-looking cooked chicken. *'Je désire le poulet, s'il vous plaît, Jacques.'*

'Vous avez bien choisi, docteur. C'est excellent! My brother brought this chicken from his farm today and my wife cooked it immediately. Very fresh.' Jacques looked enquiringly at his customer. *'Et avec ça?* Anything else?'

'C'est tout, merci. That's all, thank you.'

The proprietor began to wrap the chicken. 'You are entertaining tonight perhaps?'

'Just a colleague from the hospital,' Pierre said quickly.

Jacques smiled as he handed over the chicken. He'd noticed the heightened colour as the doctor had spoken. Such a nice young man, but it was sad he had no wife. He hoped the colleague was a pretty nurse or lady doctor.

Jacques turned back along the main street and before long was driving up the hill towards his home. He turned into his drive and parked outside the front door.

'Papa!'

The door had opened and his son rushed out like a mini-tornado. 'You missed the end of the story. Jacky finished it, but she'll tell it again, won't you, Jacky?'

'Later perhaps if your papa wants to hear it.'

Jacky was smiling, looking more relaxed than Pierre had ever seen her as she followed the small whirlwind out to the car.

He lifted his son high in the air before putting him back on the ground and kissing him on both cheeks. Jacky stood back, feeling like an intruder as she watched this happy family unit. Pierre, as if sensing her discomfort, moved forward and took both her hands in his.

'Thank you so much, Jacky,' he said in English as he kissed her on both cheeks in the French way of greeting friends.

Jacky knew that was all it was. It was the way Pierre greeted all his guests. But on this occasion it meant so much to her. She felt included at last. She wasn't an outsider any more.

'Did Nadine give you supper before she left, Christophe?' Pierre asked as he led the way into the house.

'*Eh bien, Papa*…well, not really.'

Pierre grinned as he made his way to the kitchen. He'd been expecting an answer like that.

'What you mean is you had supper ages ago, you're starving again and you'd like to have supper with Jacky and me. *N'est-ce pas?*'

'Papa! How did you know?'

'Because that's what you always say when you want to stay up late.'

'But tomorrow it's Saturday so I don't have to go to school, do I?'

'No, you don't,' Pierre said, as his mind switched to

the problem of what he would do if Nadine didn't return tonight.

He would think about that later. Right now he had to produce some supper.

'But first a glass of wine,' he said, reaching into the fridge where he pulled out a bottle of Chablis.

Quickly uncorking it, he looked round to give a glass to Jacky. Christophe had taken her back to the terrace and was proudly showing her the pictures he'd drawn.

Pierre carried the bottle in one hand and the glasses in the other. Supper could wait a while. He loved to see his son so happy…even if he was storing up problems to be dealt with at a later date.

He handed a glass of wine to Jacky. 'Come and sit down for a few minutes, Jacky. Christophe, would you like to draw another picture you can show to Jacky when she's had time for a drink?'

'OK.' The little boy picked up a bright red crayon and looked out across the garden before starting to draw the sun that was slowly sinking behind the trees. The end of the garden was lit up with a huge golden glow that Christophe found very exciting as he swept his crayons boldly across the paper.

Pierre positioned a couple of chairs where they could look out across the garden to the sea beyond.

'It's the most glorious view you have here,' Jacky said, as she sank down against the cushions and took a sip of her wine.

'I know. That's what drew me to the house. That and the fact that it was so convenient for the hospital.'

They both sat very still in a companiable silence as they watched the sunset. As the last rays disappeared into the sea and twilight descended, Pierre pressed a switch and hidden lights appeared along the terrace.

Jacky found the beauty of the evening almost took her breath away. It was a long time since she'd felt so at peace with herself.

'I've finished my picture,' Christophe said, running along the terrace, clutching the piece of paper.

He gave it first to Jacky who declared it was beautiful and a true likeness of what had just happened. Pierre admired the bright red of the sun and the brown trees with the bold yellow stripes on them.

'I didn't have any gold so I used my yellow crayon.'

'I'll put it on the kitchen wall,' Pierre said, standing up. 'Let's all go and get supper ready.'

'Papa, may I watch a video until supper is ready?' Christophe was already making his way to the small playroom off the kitchen, sure that his father would be too busy to mind what he did.

'OK, but you must come as soon as I call you.'

Arriving in the kitchen, Pierre pulled the cooked chicken from its wrapper.

'The *charcuterie* in St Martin was just about to close but the owner said he could wait another five minutes,' Pierre said. 'He knows me very well now. I'm always his last customer of the evening.'

He unwrapped the chicken and placed it on a large blue and white serving dish.

'Would you like me to make a salad?' Jacky asked.

'Yes, please, do. There's some salad in the fridge and the wine vinegar and olive oil is in that cupboard. Help yourself to herbs from those pots on the window-sill. And there should be some spinach soup in the fridge, unless Nadine and Christophe have eaten it all…'

'*Non, Papa*,' Pierre called from the playroom. 'We had omelette for supper…not very much. I'm very hungry again.'

'I'm sure you are,' Pierre said, smiling as he went over to the fridge to search for the soup.

Jacky was kneeling down, removing the lettuce from a lower shelf. Their hands touched as he located the soup container. He turned to look at her and his heart seemed to stand still. She looked so serene as she performed her homely tasks. Was it just that he hadn't met anyone like this since Liliane had died? Just now he felt he'd never met anyone who could rouse such deep emotion inside him.

On the spur of the moment, he leaned forward and very gently, kissed the side of her cheek.

Quickly he pulled himself up to his full height. Jacky was smiling up at him, her lovely hair fanning out across her shoulders, making her look like the young girl he remembered from way, way back.

'You're doing a great job, Jacky,' he said in English as he closed the fridge door.

Jacky gave a self-deprecating shrug. 'I'm only making a salad, for heaven's sake. It's not rocket science or—'

'I don't mean that. It's…it's just being here that's made all the difference this evening,' he said huskily.

He turned away and quickly reverted to French before he revealed too much of his true feelings. All his sensual feelings were impossibly aroused just by being near her. Impossibly, because he couldn't bring himself to move into a more tantalisingly dangerous situation with this siren who'd bewitched him against his will…or could he?

She'd probably bewitched him unknowingly. Certainly without any kind of planning on her part. She wasn't that kind of woman. She'd always appeared so self-sufficient and cheerful after she'd coped with the traumas in her life. It was up to him to show how he felt…which was…? Confused!

One thing was for sure. He was beginning to feel like throwing caution to the winds. And the evening had barely started! This was the domestic bit, the easy, uncomplicated section of the evening where he could pretend to be the long-lost friend who couldn't possibly pose a threat to the girl from the village where they'd spent…or misspent…their youth.

How would he cope when, after he'd put Christophe to bed, the two of them were alone and his urge to take Jacky in his arms grew even more intense?

'I made this spinach soup last night about midnight,' he said, quickly trying to get himself back on course as he tipped the contents of the container into a large saucepan before setting it on top of the cooker.

Keep on talking about mundane things, he told himself. And speak English because you'll have to work harder on what you're saying. Ignore your sexual urges. It will pass if you concentrate on making supper. Afterwards will be the testing point but for the moment just keep talking…

He cleared his throat. 'I've inherited a vegetable patch at the back of the house so I had to keep on the gardener who's been working here for years. Last night he presented me with a huge basketful of spinach…that's the right word for *épinards*, isn't it?'

Jacky smiled. 'Your English is perfect tonight, Pierre. I'm glad you're giving me a break after I've been speaking French all day.'

He found himself relaxing as he felt some of the emotional and physical pressure disappearing. He felt almost normal again.

'I hope you like spinach, Jacky. I'll add a dash of cream to make it more interesting…' He was stirring the pan now. Concentrating on the movements of the wooden spoon helped. Jacky would have no idea of the erotic thoughts going through his mind!

'I'm very impressed with your culinary expertise, Dr Mellanger,' Jacky said as she mixed her vinaigrette. 'You obviously enjoy cooking.'

'Hah! I hated it at first. My mother always kept me out of the kitchen. She waited on my father and me as if cooking were a mysterious art that a mere man couldn't possibly comprehend.'

He hesitated. 'Liliane didn't cook much so we ate out or lived off take-aways.'

There! He hadn't felt a thing when he'd spoken about her. That was a first! He was improving. Spurred on, he thought he'd confide some more. Jacky was a good listener and talking about Liliane always helped to get rid of some of the mystique surrounding his marriage. For years he'd shied away from talking about what had really happened between them.

'After Liliane died I decided to find out what cooking was all about. I figured it couldn't be more difficult than surgery. Oh, I don't want to go into the cordon bleu category. Perish the thought! For the brilliant stuff I go to a good restaurant. At home I take short cuts all the time, like buying my chicken ready cooked when I'm late home, as I did tonight. But when I have a day off or somebody to cook for, I enjoy making a special effort. You must come round some time when I've had long enough to really prepare something interesting.'

'Do you often entertain?' Jacky asked in an innocent tone as she rummaged through the cutlery drawer to find what she needed to set the kitchen table.

She'd found it hard enough listening to Pierre talking about his life with Liliane. But that was all in the past. What she wanted to know was who Pierre brought back for supper in the present! Which of her colleagues had been invited here and—what was more important—how romantic had the evening been after they'd had supper? Had they…?

'I haven't got around to inviting people back here yet,' Pierre said, picking up a sharp knife to carve the chicken. 'Haven't had much time to spare since I settled in.'

Jacky placed the cutlery on the table and began laying it out. She felt an enormous sense of relief. 'So I'm honoured to be here tonight.'

Pierre smiled as he stuck a fork in the chicken and began carving. 'Yes, you're the first.'

He put down the knife and looked across the table at his guest. Jacky was more than an honoured guest. He couldn't define what he felt about her. He'd known her all his life, it seemed. Even the years when they'd been apart he'd often remembered the wild, exciting girl who'd really captured his imagination with her flowing, flame-coloured hair and her air of devil may care. Now, with the same, albeit somewhat modified characteristics, he was finding her irresistible.

He moved round the table and put a hand lightly on her shoulder. She paused, putting down the spoon she was holding as she turned to look up at him enquiringly. She seemed puzzled, but there was something else. In her eyes he thought he could see mirrored the same kind of desire he was feeling.

At least, he hoped he could. Perhaps he was deluding himself but he was going to take a chance. He bent his head and kissed her on the lips. Her lips were parted, almost as if waiting for his kiss. *Mon Dieu!*

Jacky felt her sensual emotions leaping to life as their kiss deepened. Her treacherous body was responding in a way that she'd never thought would happen again. She shouldn't allow herself to go along with this feeling. If she gave in to the erotic sensations that Pierre's caresses were arousing…

'*Papa, est-ce que le diner…?*' Christophe ambled into the kitchen, rubbing his eyes sleepily.

They sprang apart, smiling at each other conspiratorially like a couple of young lovers caught *in flagrante delicto*.

Jacky was glad that Pierre was still holding her hand. She would let herself down slowly from the heavenly sensations she'd been experiencing. The sensual vibes were still flowing between them. She'd been hungry when she'd arrived here this evening. She was still hungry, but not for food.

She realised it was the same sensual hunger born of a deep, incomprehensible frustration that had been with her ever since she'd first seen Pierre all those years ago. If fate had brought them finally together, if fate intended them to be lovers, then why were there so many obstacles strewn in the path ahead? Why did she get the impression that Pierre was irrevocably attached to his wife? And she herself was permanently traumatised by the events of the past and the shadow they cast on any future relationship.

If only they could have got together when they'd been young adults, before the sorrows of their lives had built up so many barriers to their happiness together. Now, that would have been some union! But now… It was too late now. She must remember that and stop fantasising about what might have been.

'OK, Christophe,' Pierre said, moving towards his son and lifting him up into his arms. 'Where would you like to sit at the table?'

'Next to Jacky,' the little boy said sleepily.

Finally, they were settled at the table, Christophe sitting on two cushions so that he could reach his plate.

'*Papa, je n'aime pas les épinards.* I don't like spinach. *Je désire un tout petit peu de poulet, s'il vous plaît.*'

As requested, Pierre put a small piece of chicken, adding a little salad, on his son's plate before serving the soup for Jacky and himself. Jacky placed the baguette in the middle of the table, helping herself and Christophe to a couple of chunks.

She dipped a piece of bread into the soup. 'Fantastic soup, Pierre! And the bread's very fresh. Did you buy it on the way home?'

'No, the mobile boulangerie calls here morning and evening.'

'Mmm, I love my bread in France,' Jacky said. 'But it has to be fresh, of course. The morning bread has lost its freshness by evening. My mother always used to send me to the boulangerie in the village to get the bread for supper. ''Pas avant cinq heures,'' she used to tell me.'

Pierre smiled. 'Yes, and your mother was right. Never go to the boulangerie before five in the evening. Wait until the freshly baked bread has been placed on the shelves.'

He looked across the table at Jacky. Their eyes met. It was a magical moment. There was no need for words. Pierre could feel himself falling in love. It was akin to zooming down through space…not that he'd ever done that! But he was sure that this rush of sensation to the head would be something similar.

As their eyes locked together, Jacky knew, without a doubt, that she'd always loved Pierre. Her feelings were simply growing in intensity. She'd been in love with him all her life. Seeing him again had simply fanned the flames.

'*Je n'ai plus faim, Papa,*' a little voice said. 'I'm not hungry any more.'

Christophe put his thumb in his mouth and leaned sideways to rest his head against Jacky's arm. Gently, she shifted the small boy onto her lap. He snuggled into a comfy position and closed his eyes.

'Would you like to go to bed, Christophe?' Pierre asked gently.

Christophe nodded as he sucked quietly on his thumb.

Pierre stood up and reached towards Jacky to take his son in his arms. As she released her grip on the little boy, he turned his head and sleepily asked her to come with him. Jacky looked enquiringly at Pierre, who was nodding his head.

'I think Christophe will settle better if you come up with us. He's very fond of you already,' he whispered.

For a brief moment a dart of anxiety shot through Pierre. He shouldn't have allowed this idyllic, cosy feeling of happy families to creep up on them this evening. But he was too happy to think about the consequences at the moment. If it was what Jacky wanted, too, he was going to give in to the temptations that he knew he couldn't resist any more. At least for tonight. For now, he wasn't going to look into the future...

Pierre tucked the sheet around little Christophe and kissed the side of his cheek. His son had managed to stay awake long enough for a short session in the bathroom, but now he was sleeping soundly. He wouldn't wake up again until morning.

Jacky followed Pierre on to the landing, feeling a moment of apprehension. They were alone at last. Her emotions were churning. Her body was aroused, but her head was trying to tell her otherwise. Perhaps it would be safer to say that she couldn't stay any longer, that she had to...?

Pierre's arms claimed her and she ignored her misgivings. The doubts vanished from her mind as she parted her lips to savour his kiss.

For a brief moment he raised his head, looking down at her with the most heart-rending, tender expression. '*Ma chérie*, I want to make love with you. But only if you…'

'Yes, oh, yes,' she whispered.

She sighed as he swept her up into his arms and carried her into his bedroom. She was barely aware of her surroundings as he laid her gently on his wide bed. The sheets had been turned back. She could feel the soft texture of the cool linen against her. She wanted to feel his body against hers…his skin…his muscles…

Jacky reached up and touched Pierre's handsome face as if to convince herself that this was really happening. She felt as if she'd been on a long journey and had finally come home. It was as if she'd always known this moment would happen. And now that it had, she was afraid that fate might do something to snatch it from her.

Pierre's hands were caressing her skin, removing everything that stood in the way of their love-making. She sighed as she felt the complete abandonment of two loving bodies entwined together, nothing between them but skin, her curves fitting into the hard, muscular curvature of Pierre's body.

His hands were exploring every part of her. She wanted to scream out that she wanted him to enter her now…now! But she sensed that the longer he tantalised her, the more heavenly it would be when their bodies fused together as one…

She opened her eyes, staring up at the unfamiliar ceiling. The light by the strange bedside illuminated the white sheet that was covering her naked body. She stretched her legs languidly. Oh, the feeling of sensuality that simply moving her limbs was giving her! She'd been fashioned from some kind of sensual fabric where every movement sent erotic tingles down her spine.

'Ah!' As she positioned herself against the soft down pillow behind her head she wondered who'd just made that ecstatic exclamation. It must have been her because Pierre was still sleeping like a baby.

She remembered his tenderness and his concern for her. She'd barely noticed when he'd slipped on a condom. Her obstetrician had told her that her chances of pregnancy, even if she were to undergo extensive surgery, were extremely remote. But even so, she was still afraid of getting pregnant.

She hadn't wanted to have a physical relationship with anyone since Paul had left her, so contraception hadn't been necessary...until tonight. Until she'd allowed herself to make love with the man she'd always wanted to be part of her life.

She put a hand behind her head as she remembered the heavenly feelings she'd experienced when their bodies had joined. When Pierre had first entered her she knew she'd never experienced such ecstasy. The vibrancy of their bodies moving together in perfect harmony had been the nearest thing to heaven that she could imagine.

Pierre stirred in his sleep, then opened his eyes. He put out his hand and drew her into his arms.

Gently, tantalisingly, he began to caress her again. Her desire matched his arousal perfectly. She sighed as the steady, rhythmic, heavenly love-making began again. There was no tomorrow. Only tonight mattered.

CHAPTER FIVE

As THE first grey light of dawn outlined the window, Pierre opened his eyes. He was feeling so happy, so complete, so… If only he could stop this awful feeling of guilt creeping up on him again. He turned his head and looked at the beautiful sleeping Jacky, her lovely hair, like spun gold, spread out across the pillow next to him. What an incredible woman to wake up to!

He closed his eyes but it was Liliane's image that now appeared in his mind. He could almost hear her voice…very worried it had been that day when she'd asked him whether they should start a family. She wasn't sure she had enough maternal instinct, but he'd been sure that maternal instinct would come with the baby. He'd told her his mother, a trained midwife, had always said that babies brought their own love with them and had convinced her she would enjoy having a baby of her own. And then…

He groaned aloud as the memories flooded back.

Jacky's eyes opened and she turned towards him, moving nearer to touch his face with her hand.

'Pierre, what is it? I thought I heard you… There is something the matter, isn't there?'

He drew her into the circle of his arms, breathing in the early morning scent of her body as she snuggled against him. If only life was so simple! Loving and being loved with no feelings of regret or guilt to haunt you.

'Tell me what's worrying you, Pierre,' she whispered.

'I shouldn't have made love to you, Jacky. I…'

'But I wanted to make love! It was a mutual feeling between us and—'

'Jacky, *ma chérie*. It was wonderful to be with you all night. I wish…I wish we could make love every night together, but…'

'You haven't got over Liliane, have you?' Jacky said quietly.

She disentangled herself from his arms and moved away to lean back against the pillows. Staring up at the alabaster ceiling, she felt strangely calm. The ceiling had some carved doves around the central light fixture, she noticed. A true romantic like herself must have designed it. This was the perfect romantic setting for the night they'd just spent together. But now it was over.

'The problem is, I feel so guilty,' Pierre said in a sombre tone, as he ran his hands through his tousled hair. 'You see, it was my fault that Liliane died.'

Jacky turned to look at him. 'What do you mean? How could you possibly be held responsible for…?'

'I persuaded Liliane that we should have a baby. She said she didn't think she had enough maternal instinct.'

Pierre jumped out of bed, shrugging into the toweling robe that he'd tossed onto the carpet at the side of the bed. Walking barefoot over to the window, he leaned his hands against the sill, staring out into the first light of day that was bringing the garden to life again. A small rabbit was sitting at the side of the garden, nibbling on something—probably a lettuce leaf from the vegetable patch.

Beyond the garden, a mist hung over the sea. Somewhere in the mist the sun was trying to shine through. Somewhere in his thoughts he was trying to find a glimmer of hope in the complicated situation he'd got himself into.

Jacky watched in silence. Although he looked calm, she

could see that Pierre was undergoing some kind of life-changing crisis.

Pierre turned from the window to look at her. 'I owe you an explanation, Jacky.' He hesitated before continuing. 'You see, when Liliane died giving birth to Christophe I felt she'd made the ultimate sacrifice that a wife could ever make. She'd given me the child I so much wanted…but at what cost. I wasn't even there to help her. I…'

His voice was choking as he put his head in his hands.

Jacky pulled back the sheet and hurried across to Pierre. He lifted his head to gaze down at her, opening his arms to hold her against him.

'Oh, Jacky,' he murmured huskily.

She shivered, realizing that she should have pulled on a robe because the morning was still chilly. But her only thought had been to bring some comfort to the distraught Pierre. She couldn't bear to see him looking so sad after they'd been so deliriously happy together during the night.

'You're cold, my love,' he said in English, opening his robe and enveloping the two of them in it as he looked down at her.

As her skin began to warm against his body, she could feel her desire stirring again. Her skin against Pierre's. She mustn't give in to her desires until she'd helped Pierre to sort out his problem.

She looked up at him and sighed. 'I realize that Liliane made the ultimate sacrifice. But it wasn't your fault. You weren't to know that there would be a problem with the birth. And she'd agreed to have a baby, hadn't she?'

'Yes, we talked it through. She was a strong-willed, independent woman, but in the end she said she'd give it a try as I was so keen on the idea. I told her she wouldn't regret her decision. I assured her that we'd share all the childcare, but…it wasn't to be.'

'I can imagine how you felt when…Liliane died,' Jacky said gently. 'I can see why—'

'I told myself that I would stay faithful to her all my life. I vowed that I wouldn't lose my heart to anyone ever again, but…'

She waited, feeling his arms tightening around her. His body was responding to the nearness of her.

'Last night was so wonderful,' he whispered. 'It was…too wonderful. I almost persuaded myself that I was free again and…'

She put her arms around his neck, drawing his head down to kiss him on the lips, desperate to give him the comfort and love he needed.

She gazed up into his eyes, wondering how she could replace his anguished expression with the *joie de vivre* that had always surrounded him in those far-off days before life had dealt him a raw deal.

'Pierre,' she whispered, 'you mustn't feel guilty. Liliane decided to go ahead and have a baby. She was an intelligent adult, she must have weighed up the pros and cons and made the decision for herself. Strong-willed people like Liliane don't go along with life-changing plans just to please somebody else, however much they may love them.'

She saw his eyes flicker momentarily, as if her words had struck a chord. She moved on relentlessly, anxious to drive home what she perceived to be the reality of the situation.

'Pierre, you've suffered for five years. Don't you think it's time you began to put yourself first and move on?'

She stepped back. He moved to take her hands in his,

leading her back to the bed. 'Jacky, last night I really believed I had the right to move on and—'

'Well, then, don't go back!'

He drew her down on to the bed beside him. His hands caressed her face, moving downwards to her bare shoulders, before lingering on her breasts as she strained against him.

'This feels so right,' he murmured as he covered her body with his. 'It's as if we were made for each other.'

As his body flared with passion he obliterated the nagging doubts from his consciousness. Later…much later, he would come back to reality…

The sun was streaming through the windows when Pierre awoke again. He felt strangely calm. He remembered how anguished he'd felt before they'd made love. But if he could put his thoughts of guilt to one side—even temporarily—then Jacky and he could be lovers. But he didn't want to hurt her when the inevitable split came. She'd suffered more than any woman should when her husband had left her and her baby had died.

He wanted so much to make her whole again, to see the emotional scars healing. He didn't want to add any further anguish to her life. But she would want more than he had to offer if they continued like this. She wouldn't want to be his temporary lover. She deserved better than that. She should be with someone who could give her everything that life had to offer.

He sighed as he realized that he could never erase the doubts that haunted him. And he didn't want Jacky to suffer because of him. The sooner he made her see the real truth of the situation, the better it would be for her.

Jacky stirred in her sleep, then opened her eyes. He leaned across and drew her against him.

'That was wonderful,' he whispered. 'And everything you said about getting rid of my guilty feelings seemed to make sense—while we were together. But…'

Jacky remained silent as she waited for him to continue.

He drew in his breath. 'I'm not sure I could completely forget the vows I made and move on. I want to have a loving, meaningful relationship with you, Jacky. I want us to be lovers, but deep down I know it could only be temporary and—'

'Pierre, I could never be part of another permanent relationship,' she said quietly. She swallowed hard. 'So we both have the same problem. You see, I won't be having any more children and so it wouldn't be fair to go into a permanent relationship knowing that I couldn't—'

'But, *chérie*!' He held her closer. 'When your emotional scars have healed you may decide you want children.'

'No, no! You see, I was injured by a patient who struck me in the abdomen when I was eight months pregnant and—'

'No. You must have—'

'That's why I went into labour…that's why my baby died two hours after he was born…' Her voice broke.

'I'm here for you, my love,' he whispered.

She choked back her tears as she attempted again to explain what had happened. 'When I was finally allowed to leave the hospital my obstetrician told me that, because of the damage to my internal organs, my chances of conceiving another child were very remote. He said that extensive surgery at a later date might improve my chances of conceiving but the birth would be difficult.'

'Oh, my darling, I hadn't realized the extent of your suffering.'

He held her close, stroking her hair until she'd finished trembling.

She lifted her head as she heard the sound of little Christophe calling out from the adjacent bedroom.

Quickly, she moved out of the circle of Pierre's arms. 'Time to go,' she whispered.

He moved round and caught her in his arms as she stepped out of bed. 'Are you sure you're all right, Jacky? Don't go if—'

'I prefer to go now, Pierre.'

'But let me at least take you home in the car.'

'I'll be fine. Please, don't worry about me, Pierre.'

She hurried across to the *en suite* bathroom before he could remonstrate with her. As she closed the door she told herself that Pierre had enough problems of his own without worrying about hers.

Her clothes were strewn across the floor. She pulled them on. She would shower when she got home. She didn't want to complicate matters by being around at breakfast-time. It would be lovely to spend more time in this wonderful family environment, but she didn't fancy answering questions from Christophe. Five-year-olds were notoriously inquisitive.

She could hear that Pierre had gone to his son's bedroom. They were laughing about something. She peeped out into Pierre's room. The coast was clear. She made a quick getaway down the stairs and out through the kitchen door.

A car was pulling into the drive, coming around the side of the house. Nadine climbed out and looked across at her.

'*Bonjour*, Dr Manson.'

Nadine showed no surprise at seeing Jacky leaving the

house at this early hour of the morning. Jacky decided to act as if the situation were perfectly normal.

She smiled. '*Bonjour*, Nadine. How is your boyfriend?'

'He's had an operation to fix his broken leg. The doctor says he will be able to leave hospital in a few days with a plaster on his leg and he's feeling much better this morning. Thank you so much for looking after Christophe for me.'

'That's OK. I'm so glad it wasn't too serious. Pierre will be relieved that you've returned.'

'Dr Mellanger can always be sure I will not let him down,' the nanny said firmly as she went in through the kitchen door.

Jacky hurried away. The weekend stretched ahead of her. She was lucky to have her off-duty at the weekend. But she knew that Pierre was working so there would be no possibility that they could get together again.

For the next couple of weeks, Jacky only saw Pierre at the hospital. There was a good rapport between them when they worked together but neither of them suggested they get together in an off-duty situation.

During the night, when she found it hard to sleep, Jacky constantly told herself the situation would work itself out. She'd met up again, after all these years, with the man who'd been her idol since childhood. That in itself was a miracle! Something she could never have imagined in her wildest dreams. And the fact that she'd spent one fabulous night with Pierre was a memory she would treasure for the rest of her life.

One hot morning in August, when the air-conditioning appeared unable to cope with the heat wave, Jacky found herself treating two patients at once. There was a young man who'd fallen under the wheels of a bus and sustained a head injury. As she was studying the injuries on the cranial scan, Marie arrived to say she needed help with another patient.

'Jacky, leave the head injury patient to me. I'm going to move him to Intensive Care. There's a complicated case just arrived. I've bleeped Pierre but he's in Theatre at the moment. Can you take a look at my new patient?'

Jacky moved swiftly across to the treatment room where the patient was being wheeled in.

'What happened?' she asked the paramedic who was handing her the case notes.

'Apparently, Monsieur Lanvin was painting the kitchen ceiling. He'd put the chairs upside down on the table to give more space for the ladder. The ladder turned and he fell onto an upturned chair leg, which impaled him in the lower region of the body.'

Jacky suppressed a shudder as she looked down at her patient. It was a blessing that he was unconscious, Jacky thought as she pulled back the sheet to examine his injuries. After a thorough examination of the injured tissues, her initial assessment was that the rectum had been damaged and the bladder perforated. It was going to require some skilful surgery if her patient was to survive.

Jacky prepared a syringe so that she could take a blood sample. He would need a transfusion as quickly as possible. She spoke quietly to the nurse who was assisting her.

'Our patient has lost a lot of blood. Take this sample to the path lab as quickly as possible. Grouping and cross-matching immediately, please. Let me know how soon they have Monsieur Lanvin's blood group.'

She fixed a line into her patient's arm so that she could begin replacing some of the fluids he'd lost with dextrose.

The door swung open. 'I came as quickly as I could.'

Jacky looked up, relieved that Pierre had arrived. Briefly, she filled him in on the case history. Together they checked on some of the details that had been written in his notes on arrival. His wife had arrived with him, apparently, but had returned to look after the children at home.

'Charles Lanvin, age thirty-two,' Pierre read out before examining their patient. 'He's going to need a colostomy, at least temporarily until we've repaired the rectum and the colon. Hopefully, the colostomy will be reversed when the injuries have healed, but…'

He straightened up and looked across the examination couch at Jacky. 'I'll phone Marcel and see if he can schedule the operation as soon as possible. The sooner we can repair the damage to the rectum and bladder, the higher chance of survival he's got.'

He was moving across to the phone on the wall. 'Marcel, I've got a patient who needs urgent attention… Yes, I understand, but the problem is…'

The nurse arrived back, breathless. 'We're in luck. The path lab had some packed cells waiting for another patient with exactly the same blood group. We can start off with these two and the lab will replace them in time for the other patient.'

'Excellent!' Jacky switched her patient's IV from dextrose to blood. As she straightened up, the patient opened his eyes and stared at her.

'What's happening?' he asked in a faint voice.

Jacky took hold of her patient's hand. 'You're in hospital, Charles. You had a fall. How are you feeling now?'

'I can't feel very much at all,' her patient said. 'Are my legs OK? They don't seem to be there any more.'

'Your legs haven't been injured,' Jacky said carefully. 'But you've hurt the lower part of your body, so we're going to take you to the operating theatre to treat the injuries.'

'I can't feel the lower part of my body at all, Doctor. I think my arms are OK,' he said uncertainly.

'Show me how you can move your arms,' Jacky said gently.

Charles lifted both arms in the air and moved his fingers.

Jacky smiled. 'That's fine.'

'Yes, but what's happened down there?'

Pierre had just returned from the phone. He put a hand on Jacky's arm. 'Let me explain.'

Jacky held her patient's hand as Pierre explained the extent of the injuries. Charles fixed his eyes on her face as he listened to what Pierre was saying. At the end of the explanation the patient ran a hand through his damp hair.

'Sounds like I've made a real mess of things. Well, I'm glad I can't feel anything down there. Will the feeling come back when you've operated on me?'

Jacky glanced at Pierre. Pierre hesitated before answering the difficult question. 'I've asked the neurological consultant to come and see you. He should be here shortly. He might be able to assess whether the loss of sensation in your lower body is temporary or permanent.'

Charles held tightly to Jacky's hand as he stifled a sob. 'We'll do everything we can to make you well again,' she said reassuringly. 'The loss of sensation could well be temporary. It sometimes happen with extreme trauma that the sensation goes but then returns.'

'I'll try to think positively,' the patient murmured. 'Where's my wife?'

'She had to return home to look after the children,'

Jacky said. 'But she'll be back as soon as she's arranged for someone to take over from her.'

The neurological consultant came into the treatment room. Jacky moved away and was immediately asked to see another newly arrived patient. A young boy in the next cubicle had fallen off his bicycle. From the unnatural angle of the leg she could see at once that the tibia was fractured. Definitely the tibia and possibly the fibula as well. Another case for the X-ray department.

'So, what happened to you?' she asked, in a sympathetic voice.

'I was going down the hill towards the sea and a cat rushed across in front of me. I swerved and…'

'I'll clean up this bit where you've cut yourself,' Jacky said, reaching for some sterile gauze from the dressings trolley. 'I'll need to stop the bleeding now and a couple of stitches will help it to heal better. I'm going to put some nice cold numbing liquid around the cut so you'll only feel me tickling the skin a little… OK? So how old are you, Daniel?'

'Nine…but I'm nearly ten.'

'And where do you go to school?'

The young boy said he was on holiday from Paris. He was still at one of the primary schools on the outskirts of Paris.

Jacky chatted as she sutured the boy's leg, trying hard to gain his confidence. It was always a relief when she found a young frightened patient relaxing. It made everything so much easier for patient and doctor.

As the day wore on, she found herself looking forward to the evening. She hadn't anything planned. She went along to her office to check for messages on the computer, replying to the urgent stuff and deciding to leave the rest until the next morning.

She switched off the computer and leaned her elbows on the desk. She felt very tired after her long day. She put her head down on her hands and closed her eyes as she realized she hadn't even taken a break at lunchtime. And it had been so hot! Somebody would have to do something about the air-conditioning before the weather got any hotter.

Yes, tonight she simply wanted to chill out with the new novel she'd bought at the local newsagent on the main street of St Martin as she'd walked to the hospital that morning. She would buy a baguette on her way home and make a *tartine au fromage* with that beautifully ripe Camembert. She didn't feel like cooking.

'Jacky, are you OK?' said a voice in English.

She opened her eyes and raised her head. 'Sorry, I didn't hear you come in, Pierre. I was…I was feeling tired…but I'm fine…really.'

In two strides he'd come across the small room. He was standing beside her, surveying her with a worried expression.

'Are you sure you don't want me to check you out? Oh, dear, my English isn't as good as it used to be. What I meant was…' He was smiling down at her now. 'I was speaking medically when I said I might check you out, of course.'

'Of course you were.' Jacky gave him a mischievous grin. 'What a pity!'

Pierre smiled as he leaned down to take both her hands in his so that he could draw her to her feet. For a few moments he stood gazing down at her with the sort of expression that made her turn weak at the knees.

Jacky could bear the tension no longer. Two weeks without even a kiss had been an impossible strain on her emotions. She raised her lips towards his. Slowly, he bent his head and their lips blended together as if they'd never been apart.

As Jacky drew back to catch her breath she looked up at Pierre.

'So what's the diagnosis, Doctor? Do you still need to check me out?'

Pierre gave her a rakish grin. 'Most definitely! How about tonight? I'll need to check your heart rate. It seemed OK just now but I'm going to prescribe a walk through the sand dunes just to make sure. Then a light picnic while we watch the sun dropping down into the sea...' He broke off.

'I'm sorry. I was presuming you're free this evening, Jacky. I should have checked first. Have you got something planned for tonight?'

'Nothing that won't keep until a later date,' she said, moving closer.

He took her in his arms again and she didn't resist as he held her close. Over the top of her head she could hear him murmuring in a seductive voice. Her treacherous body was already melting at the prospect of a whole evening together. She didn't feel the least bit tired any more. Besides, it would be so relaxing, simply sitting amongst the sand dunes watching the sun go down...

'If I've seemed a little distracted since you spent the night with me,' he whispered huskily, reverting to French so that he could express himself more easily, 'it's because I've been doing a lot of thinking. And I've come to the conclusion that this kind of feeling that we have between us...'

He broke off, so she raised her head and kissed him briefly. 'You were saying, Doctor...'

He smiled down at her. 'This kind of feeling that exists between us whenever we're together can't be wrong.'

Even as he said this, the nagging part of his brain clicked in, reminding him of the vow he'd made five years ago. He tried to banish the thought. He could try to rationalize his problem away but he could never forget it.

He took a deep breath. Even if this problem was always going to be with him, even if the nightmares concerning Liliane were going to plague him from time to time, he felt sure he was meant to experience a loving affair with Jacky. However brief it was, he was going to make sure she wouldn't regret it. Hopefully, in giving his love to her he could help to heal some of her emotional scars too.

Jacky ran her finger over his forehead, obliterating the frown lines that so frequently appeared when they were together.

'Try not to worry,' she said quietly.

She moved away from him and sat down at her desk. She began clearing away the pile of papers she'd meant to sort out before she went off duty but was now relegating to tomorrow's work list.

Pierre turned at the door. 'How soon can you be ready?'

She looked up from her desk. 'Give me half an hour. How about you? Won't you have to go home to see Christophe?'

'I told you that Nadine's boyfriend Guy was now out of hospital, didn't I?'

Jacky nodded. 'Yes, he was only in for a couple of days, wasn't he?'

'Yes. He sustained a fractured tibia which needed a plate to strengthen the injured area. He's getting around fine on crutches at the moment. Nadine asked if he could come to stay with us to convalesce.'

'I remember you told me. It seems like a good arrangement. While Nadine can have Guy with her, she won't be worrying.'

'Exactly! And I don't have to worry that Nadine will be leaving us to go back to Paris. He's even talking about moving over to St Martin and looking for a job when his leg has healed.'

Jacky smiled. 'So the arrangement is working out very well?'

'It's a great relief for all of us. Nadine and Guy have taken Christophe out for the day to Nausica, the marine theme park. They won't be back until late this evening and Nadine said she would put Christophe to bed when they returned.'

'So, we've got plenty of time to enjoy ourselves this evening.'

'We certainly have.'

CHAPTER SIX

PIERRE parked the car outside the *charcuterie*. 'Do you want to come inside and help me chose the picnic, Jacky?'

'Of course. I'd love to.' She put her hand on the door-handle but Pierre had hurried round to open it for her, holding out his hand to clasp hers as she stepped on to the pavement.

The delicious aromas of French delicatessens were one of the joys of living in France as far as Jacky was concerned. And to have the money to buy whatever she chose! Unlike when she'd been a child! It would be so easy to put together a picnic from the mouthwatering products on display. The problem would be in limiting the choice so that they didn't have too much to carry.

The owner of the shop came forward with a welcoming smile for the handsome couple.

Pierre's hand was on Jacky's waist as he introduced her. 'Jacques, this is Dr Jacky Manson, one of my colleagues at the hospital, and a very dear friend from the village where I was born. I've known her since she was a child.'

Jacques came round the counter so that he could get a better look at Jacky. *'Enchanté, madame.'* He turned towards Pierre. 'Was your friend as beautiful as this when she was a child?'

Pierre grinned. 'Of course! But she was much younger than me so I didn't appreciate her beauty in those far-off days.'

Pierre put his credit card on the counter. 'I'm going to

leave it to Jacky to choose some food for a picnic. I suspect she's better at this sort of thing than me.'

Jacky laughed. 'I love spending money on food. I warn you, I shall buy more than we need.'

Pierre smiled. 'Good, because I'm starving.'

'That makes two of us,' Jacky said happily as she surveyed the mouthwatering scene. 'I'll start with some *pâté de foie gras*. That was always way above my family's budget. Quatre cent grammes, s'il vous plaît, Jacques. Et avec ça…'

Jacques's wife had arrived from the kitchen at the back of the shop and had to be introduced. She was carrying freshly baked *quiche aux asperges*. Jacky loved asparagus quiche and immediately appropriated one. Madame put it in a special waxed carton so that it wouldn't spoil during transit.

Pierre stood back, pleased that Jacky had taken control of the arrangements. He was also pleased to see her so happy again. He had a sudden memory of seeing her once, as a small child, pressing her nose against the window of the charcuterie, looking at all the goods on display. And now, even though she was a medical professional, she still found delight in simple pleasures.

He picked up a bottle of claret from the wine section at the back of the shop. He'd ask Jacques if he could lend him a couple of glasses.

After several minutes they emerged from the shop, Jacky smiling like a happy child who'd just spent all her pocket money in the sweet shop.

'*Bonne soirée*,' the friendly proprietor called from the doorway.

'*Merci*, Jacques,' Pierre said as he opened the boot of the car.

'What a feast we're going to have!' Jacky said, as she

helped Pierre to load the packages. Jacques had insisted on lending them plates, glasses, a corkscrew and paper napkins.

'We'll need to have the picnic close to the car. I know just the place,' Pierre said as he started the car.

There were a couple of further stops along the street to buy a baguette and some peaches. As Pierre headed towards the sea, Jacky leaned back and luxuriated in a feeling of relaxation. An hour ago she'd been exhausted by her work at the hospital but now she felt exhilarated at the prospect of the evening with Jacques that stretched ahead.

'It's cooling down at last,' she said, as she breathed in the salty air.

Jacques put a hand on hers. 'It's going to be a perfect sunset tonight. The sun is still high in the sky but it's soon going to start setting. And then the sky will fill with those lovely shades of pink and gold. I love this time of day in summer, don't you?'

'Mmm...'

She looked out to sea as the car sped along towards the outskirts of St Martin. She loved any time of day when she was with Pierre.

Pierre turned the car down a small metalled road that soon deteriorated into a sandy track. He drove as far as he could before the track finished at the edge of some sand dunes.

He turned towards her. 'We'll find a nice spot with a good view. Somewhere over there, don't you think?'

She looked in the direction he was pointing. 'It looks perfect to me. Very quiet, which is what I need at the end of a noisy day.'

'Oh, it's quiet. We're the only people having an evening picnic. Listen…we can't hear anything but the sea rustling up onto the shore…'

He leaned forward to kiss her. She savoured the touch of his lips, the closeness. Just the two of them…

'Come on, let's move,' Pierre said, jumping over the side of his car and hurrying round to open her door.

Laden with the packages, they trekked through the soft sand towards a hollow between two dunes with an excellent view of the sea.

'Unwrapping the food is almost as much fun as buying it!' Jacky said as she began to spread everything on the large paper sheet that Jacques had given them. 'Do you know, I think it's almost worth being poor as a child so that you can appreciate all the goodies you can buy when you have some money as an adult.'

Pierre smiled. 'Jacky, I love to see you looking so happy. You always looked happy as a child even without any money to spare.'

'After my mother left home, I used to make a point of trying to look as if I was happy,' she said lightly. 'I used to smile and hope that nobody would guess how sad I was feeling.' She hesitated. 'It was much harder to remain cheerful as an adult when fate took a hand in my life but… I'm sorry to sound morbid! Let's change the subject and look forward—not backward—tonight.'

'Let's just live for the moment!'

Pierre uncorked the wine and poured a couple of glasses. 'Cheers!' he said, clinking his glass against Jacky's.

'*Santé!*' she replied, lifting the glass to her lips.

'I wonder why food tastes so much better in the open air,' Jacky said, as she pushed her plate away and wiped some peach juice from her fingers. 'That was the most yummy picnic I ever had. Oh, look! The sun is almost in the sea now. I know it's all an illusion, but as a child I used to think the sun dived into the sea and stayed there until the next morning. I couldn't think how it managed to appear again in a completely different place.'

Pierre leaned forward and put his arm around her shoulder. 'When did you find out it was all an illusion?' he asked.

'Oh, my father told me when I was about five. I was so sad he'd explained the mystery away. I used to like mysteries. Still do…'

Her voice trailed away and she looked up into Pierre's eyes. 'Perhaps that's why I like you. Because…'

'Because I'm something of a mystery?' Pierre said huskily.

She nodded. 'I don't think I really understand you. You're a very complicated person.'

Pierre sighed. 'Don't I know it! I wish I could go back to the days when life was simple. No complications…just life stretching ahead of me to do what I liked with it.'

She snuggled closer. 'Make a wish now. Now, while the sun is sinking into the sea. It's a·magical time. Can't you feel the magic all around us? Maybe the mythical sun god will go to visit the sea god while he's down in the sea during the night and…'

Pierre smiled fondly as he looked down at her. 'Jacky, you're so wonderful! Whenever you find me taking myself too seriously, I'd like you to make up a funny story like you did just now.'

She looked up at him, feeling happy that she seemed to be helping to heal the emotional scars that still troubled Pierre. He held her close while they watched the sun set.

'Ah!' Jacky gave a long sigh as the horizon grew dark.

Almost immediately, a pink and golden glow suffused the sky, casting its ethereal colours over the sea.

Pierre took hold of Jacky's hands and drew her to her feet.

'Let's walk down to the sea, Jacky.'

Jacky put on a mischievous grin. 'You mean we're going to go and look for the sun?'

Pierre smiled. 'Yes, let's go and find the sun again.'

'Or we could search for the moon.'

She took her hand away from Pierre's and ran as quickly as she could towards the sea.

'Whee! I'm going to get there first…'

She could hear his feet pounding behind her. It was so exhilarating running on this deserted beach, being pursued by the most wonderful man in the world. She could imagine he was a knight in shining armour, pursuing her on his horse to claim her for ever! She banished reality as she revelled in the fairy-tale romantic ideas that were swirling around in her head. It was a totally unreal situation. Pure make-believe. It wasn't really happening. The fact that she and Pierre were here alone on a deserted beach.

Pierre caught her round the waist and swept her up into his arms.

She laughed as he pulled her against him. 'My Prince Charming has arrived,' she murmured before his lips claimed hers.

She could feel desire running through her whole body. She wanted him to take her here on the beach. This was the stuff of dreams! She wanted to experience everything now. Now, while her passion was so aroused, before she had to go back to the real world.

Pierre raised his head and looked down at her. She appeared to be trembling. He wanted so much to make love to her. He was going to make sure they got together to-night. But later...

Still carrying her in his arms, he walked slowly towards the sea, kicking off his shoes as he began to wade into the water. Jacky's hands around his neck tightened.

'We're really going to look for the sun, aren't we?' she said lightly, going along with the make-believe world they'd created. 'Are you going to put me down in the water?'

Pierre stopped walking. 'That depends. If you promise to invite me back to your apartment, I'll put you down safely on the shore.' He raised one eyebrow, a rakish grin on his face. 'It's non-negotiable.'

Jacky felt a surge of pure joy running through her. There was absolutely no doubt about what Pierre had in mind.

'In that case, I accept the terms of the agreement,' she whispered. 'Let's go back now.'

As he carried her back to the shore she could feel her desire mounting. He put her down on the beach and they walked back up the beach hand in hand.

The picnic things were exactly as they'd left them. They packed the remains away and trekked back through the dunes to the car.

As he got into the car, Pierre took his mobile from his pocket to check for messages. 'I told Nadine my phone would be switched on all the time so that she can get in touch if there's a problem with Christophe. Sometimes she simply texts me.'

He put his mobile back in his pocket and started the engine. 'No news is good news. That's the English saying, isn't it? I think Nadine and Guy enjoy playing at parents with Christophe. They're very much in love. I would say marriage is definitely on the cards.'

'And then you'll have to find another nanny, won't you?'

Pierre groaned. 'Don't remind me. Nadine has been the best nanny I've employed. And I don't know how Christophe will take it when she goes.'

'It must be a worry for you, the lack of continuity in Christophe's childcare,' she said.

Pierre stared ahead at the sandy track, gripping the steering-wheel as he felt the pangs of anxiety growing again.

'That's been one of the worst problems of bringing up Christophe by myself. I was pleased for Christophe when he bonded with someone, but when that person had to move on…'

'Is that why you didn't want me to meet Christophe on that first evening?' she asked. 'I sat outside in the car and wondered why.'

'Jacky, I'm so sorry about that.' He'd negotiated the bumpy track and was now driving along the main road towards St Martin. He took one hand off the wheel and placed it over hers. 'I knew that Christophe would become attached to you…as he did as soon as you met.'

'It's OK. I understand now,'

Pierre swallowed hard. 'Christophe has been asking about you. Only yesterday he wanted to know when you were coming to the house again.'

'I miss him, too. When you and I stop seeing each other…'

'Don't talk about it!' He drew in his breath. 'We're together now and that's all that matters. I've stopped looking too far into the future when I'm with you, Jacky.'

She leaned back against her seat. 'So have I.'

*   *   *

Pierre parked the car in front of her apartment and turned to put his arm on the back of her seat. 'You're sure you want to invite me in?'

'So long as you wipe the sand from your feet before you go up the stairs.'

Pierre laughed. 'I'll do better than that. I'll take my shoes off and leave them on the mat.'

'Oh, don't do that. It's a communal entrance hall. What would my neighbours think? They would think I was entertaining a man in my apartment. I have my reputation to think about.'

'OK, I'll carry them in my hand.'

As they reached the top of the stairs, Jacky slotted her key in the door. She suddenly felt uncharacteristically nervous.

'Not very palatial but it's all I could find when I first arrived,' she began, striding across the small entrance hall, chattering to relieve the sudden tension she was feeling. 'And it's near the hospital. Let me give you the grand tour. This is the living room, this is the kitchen, this is the bedroom and the bathroom is—'

Pierre swung her round and took her into his arms. 'Tonight I'm only interested in you, *chérie*. You can show me the apartment later.'

She looked up into his eyes and revelled in the expression of tender passion she saw there.

'Let's make love,' she whispered as she led him over to the bed.

Jacky opened her eyes. The moon was shining through the uncurtained windows directly onto her. Her first thought on waking each morning was usually that she must find time to buy some curtains. It was even more important if Pierre was going to come here often.

She turned her head on the pillow. Beside her, Pierre

was still asleep, sleeping very peacefully. She could see that there was no trace of anxiety about him now. All trace of tension had disappeared.

She put a hand behind her head and lay back against her pillows. She would treasure the memories of this night for the rest of her days. If they never got together again, this one time would always be with her.

She felt a rush of sensual desire mounting inside her as she remembered the loving, tantalising way that Pierre had caressed and kissed every part of her. And as he'd thrust deeper inside her she felt as if she'd become a part of him, that they were joined together for ever...

'You're awake,' Pierre moved closer now, drawing her against him to kiss her gently on the lips.

'Do you have to go home?' she whispered, feeling that she should make the effort to come down to earth.

She had to accept that Pierre was a man with family responsibilities.

'Not yet,' he said huskily. 'Nadine would have phoned me if there was a problem with Christophe. Besides, I can't leave you without saying goodbye...'

This time, when they made love, it was with a new-found intimacy. They'd explored each other completely before and felt utterly comfortable in every movement they made. Every caress was special now and even more sensually exciting than the first time.

Jacky cried out again and again as she climaxed, clinging to Pierre, wanting him to stay and never leave her...

Pierre climbed out of bed, surveying the pile of clothes on the floor. He gave her a bemused grin. 'Looks as if I was in a terrible hurry to take you to bed.'

As Jacky lay back against the pillows she couldn't help admiring Pierre's hunky, virile body. Memories of their love-making were making her feel sexy again. She drew in her breath and told herself to get real. She really had to come down to earth now and stop fantasising.

'Would you like breakfast before you go, Pierre?'

He grinned. '*Chérie*, it's two o'clock in the morning.'

'So?'

He leaned across the bed and kissed her, his fingers lingering over her bare shoulders, sending shivers through her.

'I'd love breakfast, but I'd better go back. If I'm lucky, do you think you might give me coffee later this morning in your office?'

'Ah, that's by invitation only, as you well know,' she said facetiously as she climbed out of bed and shrugged into her robe. 'I'll have to check my desk diary when I get back on duty and let you know.'

He pulled on his clothes, before moving round the bed, still buttoning up his shirt. 'Then I'll look forward to hearing from you, Doctor.'

He drew her against him and she savoured the scent of his body, so evocative of their night of passionate love-making. As they kissed she felt as if her heart would break if this was the last time she ever saw him. Saying goodbye was always the hard bit with Pierre. But at least she knew she would see him again in a few hours. How would she possibly cope when their affair ended?

She pulled back and looked up at him. It was time to stop pretending that they were going to be with each other for ever.

'You've missed a button in the middle here,' she said, in a practical tone of voice, her fingers lingering too long over the gap where she could feel the skin over his muscular chest as she fastened the button.

'Are you OK, Jacky?' His voice was full of concern as he looked down at her.

'I'm fine!' she said brightly. 'It's time you were off. I'll see you later.'

She practically pushed him out of the bedroom towards the main door, holding it open as she watched him going down the stairs. He turned to wave as he reached the bend in the stairs and she waved back before closing the door and leaning against it.

She found she was panting as if she'd just run a race. She took a deep breath to steady her nerves. Was it worth putting herself through the agony of wondering about the future just to experience a few hours of happiness with Pierre?

Her rational side told her that it wasn't, that she was heading for trouble, storing up more anguish than even she had ever experienced. But her optimistic side was telling her to follow her heart. Keep on with the fictitious make-believe idea that this could go on for ever. Live for the moment.

She needed advice from somebody who'd suffered in similar circumstances, she told herself. And who better than her dear friend Debbie, the doctor she'd replaced? Debbie was always pleased when she called in for a gossip about hospital life and had told her about the emotional problems she and Marcel had dealt with.

Jacky had told Debbie about her relationship with Paul and the tragedy of her newborn baby. But she'd deliberately kept quiet about her relationship with Pierre. It wasn't that she didn't trust Debbie to keep a confidence, it was the fact that she herself was so unsure about her relationship with Pierre.

In fact, whenever Debbie had tried to find out what was going on, Jacky had changed the subject. On one occasion she'd said she'd rather not talk about it. And Debbie had remained silent since then, respecting her desire for privacy.

As she walked slowly back to her bedroom, she wondered if a few words of wisdom from a friend who'd been in a difficult, seemingly impossible relationship would help her. It couldn't do any harm to explain the situation and then listen to what Debbie had to say, could it?

She had a half-day off today so she could phone this morning and see if Debbie was going to be in this afternoon. Meanwhile, she had to get some sleep. She was on duty in a few hours and would need to have all her wits about her.

'Hope you weren't planning on going out this afternoon,' Jacky said as she stepped inside the beautiful house Debbie shared with her husband Marcel.

'It was a lovely surprise when you phoned this morning,' Debbie said. 'If I'd had plans I would have changed them. It's always good to see you again. Thiery is in his cot, having his afternoon sleep, so we can sit down and have a good old gossip.'

Jacky enjoyed the fact that they always spoke English together. Like her, Debbie had one English and one French parent, but they'd both lived a long time in England and English seemed the most natural language to use when they were on their own.

'May I peep at Thiery first?' Jacky asked.

'Of course you can!'

They climbed the stairs together. 'Whenever I'm here, I always think what a fabulous house this is,' Jacky said.

'It was designed by the same architect who planned Pierre's house just along the road. Don't you think the houses are similar? Especially this wide staircase and the landing.'

Jacky smiled as they reached the spacious landing. 'How would I possibly know what the stairs and landing are like in Pierre's house?' She paused with her hand on the banister at the top of the stairs. 'You're fishing, aren't you?'

Debbie laughed. 'I'm always fishing for news of your…er…relationship with Pierre. But I never get anywhere.'

Jacky hesitated. 'I've decided I need to talk to you about it today. There's absolutely nobody else I would confide in. But let me see your gorgeous baby first.'

Jacky leaned over the cot, admiring the sleeping baby. He was so wonderful! She could feel pangs of longing for the baby she'd lost. But she managed to stay calm and unmoved on the surface.

'I'd love to pick him up.'

'Oh, there'll be plenty of time to cuddle him when he wakes up. But I'm looking forward to our chat today. Marcel is scheduled for a long session in Theatre this evening so we won't be disturbed.'

'Where's Emma?'

'She's with Françoise over at her brother's farm. Jérome, Françoise's son, came to drive them over there because Emma was longing to see the new baby calf. I'm so lucky to have Françoise to help me here. Especially during the school holidays.'

'Françoise lives in, doesn't she?' Jacky said as they went down the staircase.

'Yes, she feels like part of the family now. Her son has got married and moved back into Françoise's house, but he still works at his uncle's farm.'

They had reached the high-ceilinged entrance hall

again. Debbie led the way through to the back of the house where the wide terrace looked out over the garden and beyond that to the sea.

'Sit down and rest while I get us something to drink. Would you like tea, coffee, fruit juice…?'

'Tea would be lovely. I'm feeling very English today.'

Debbie raised an eyebrow. 'Not feeling homesick, are you?'

Jacky shrugged. 'I'm equally at home in France as in England. France was where I was born and spent my childhood. But England was where…where I thought I had everything I wanted in life…for a while. I sometimes feel nostalgic for the happiness I experienced in England, even if it didn't last. But I'm not here to talk about the past—it's the present I'm concerned about.'

'I'll get the tea,' Debbie said, in a sympathetic tone. 'And then you can tell me all about it.'

As soon as they were settled with their teacups, Debbie restarted the conversation. 'So tell me how things are going with you and Pierre? Any chance the relationship is going to be permanent?'

Jacky shook her head. 'It's wonderful when we're together but I know I can't compete with Pierre's late wife. He's put her up there on a pedestal and she's always going to be there. Even though she died five years ago, he's still committed to her memory. The perfect wife! I'm only a temporary girlfriend.'

Debbie put down her cup and leaned forward. 'Jacky, I don't think she was as perfect as Pierre thinks.'

'What do you mean?'

Debbie hesitated. 'I'm not sure about this…but…it was something that Marcel started to tell me when he knew Pierre was coming to work at the hospital. He kind of hinted that Pierre had suffered a raw deal with Liliane. I don't know the details, but when Marcel was out in Australia with Pierre he suspected that Liliane was being unfaithful to Pierre.'

Jacky drew in her breath. 'No! But I always imagined she was a paragon of virtue! From what Pierre has told me about her, she couldn't possibly—'

'Oh, Pierre knew nothing about it, Jacky! That was the difficult part for Marcel. Keeping a secret that would have broken Pierre's heart.'

Jacky swallowed the lump in her throat. 'So what was this secret that Marcel discovered?'

'I wish I knew! When I started asking Marcel questions he just clammed up on me. Said he'd told me too much already. It wasn't his place to divulge something that would hurt Pierre. But now I've heard how you're suffering because Pierre is still emotionally tied to his wife, don't you think it's time that he knew the truth?'

Jacky opened her eyes wide. 'No, we can't do that!'

'Why not?'

'Because if it's something that would have broken Pierre's heart when Liliane was alive, think how much more it would affect him now, Debbie.' Jacky shook her head. 'For five years, he's cherished her memory, her unselfishness in giving him his son Christophe, making the ultimate sacrifice. No, we've got to leave Pierre with his perfect memories. I couldn't bear to see him unhappy.'

'You really love him, don't you?' Debbie said gently.

Jacky nodded. 'I've got a serious case of teenage angst, which is all the more painful when you're an adult. I'm terribly jealous of Liliane, but I don't want Pierre to become disillusioned.'

Debbie sighed in exasperation. 'But that's when you would step in and comfort him! Make yourself indispensable when he needed emotional support. He'd turn to you and before you knew it—'

'No, Debbie. Please, don't say anything because that's not the only reason why I couldn't be a permanent partner for Pierre.'

'What do you mean? Surely…'

'You know I told you about giving birth to Simon…how he died when he was just a couple of hours old…'

Debbie leaned across and squeezed Jacky's hand. 'I know you suffered a great deal but if you and Pierre were really together you could have another baby.'

'No, Debbie. My obstetrician told me that there's very little chance I could get pregnant again. Even if I underwent extensive surgery, my chances are still slim. And in the unlikely event of a pregnancy it would lead to another dangerous and traumatic birth. I made up my mind after the last time that I would never put myself through that again. So, even if Pierre did suggest we make our relationship permanent, I couldn't accept. Understanding him as I do, I know he would want more children.'

'But, Jacky—'

'So it would be unfair of me to become Pierre's permanent partner.'

'You might change your mind once—'

'No I wouldn't! I—' Jacky broke off. 'I think I can hear Thiery crying.'

'So can I.'

Jacky put on a smile. 'May I go and bring him down?'

'Of course!' Debbie hesitated. 'You're a natural with babies, Jacky.'

'Other people's!' Jacky said wryly as she went out into the hall.

Thiery was lying on his back, bawling loudly, when

she arrived at his cotside. She leaned down and lifted him gently into her arms. The crying stopped at once as the tiny face snuffled against her.

'There there, my little treasure. What's the matter? Tell Jacky what it is you want, my precious.'

The indefinable smell of baby skin brought back all the memories of Simon that she was trying to forget. She thought she'd got used to the idea that she would never have another baby, but whenever she held one in her arms, in or outside hospital, she felt broody again.

It was a feeling she was going to have to live with for the rest of her life.

CHAPTER SEVEN

AS JACKY looked out of the window of her little office in the hospital, she could see the hot sun beating down on the hospital forecourt. A few days ago, some of the tarmac had melted in the fierce August heat and workers were now repairing the damage. This meant there was less space for the ambulances to manoeuvre when they brought in patients, which caused difficulties if more than two ambulances arrived at once.

Pierre had told her that the contractors had promised to get the job done as quickly as possible but it didn't look as if the workmen were in any hurry at the moment. She turned back to her computer screen. Who could blame them for going at a slower pace in this heat wave! She was glad the air-conditioning had been fixed in the hospital.

She'd still found it difficult working in the reception area early this morning when she'd treated a patient with a bad case of sunburn who hadn't been able to sleep in the night. The doors of that part of the hospital were always open so new patients had easy access, which meant that the air-conditioning wasn't as effective.

When she'd no longer been required out there she'd escaped to her office to catch up with her paperwork. As soon as it was finished she switched off her computer. Standing up, she stretched her arms high above her head.

'That's what I like to see, someone doing their morning exercises.'

She put her arms down as Pierre came in. He strode

towards her and held out his hands. She took hold of them and stayed absolutely still, revelling in the sensual electric current running between them.

It had only been a few hours since Pierre had left her bed and it had been hard to start work this morning. But the difficult transition from lover to medical colleague was always worth making so that she could enjoy the heavenly experience of having Pierre with her for a few hours.

During the last few weeks, since they'd spent that evening on the beach watching the sunset, their romance had deepened into something exquisitely poignant. She couldn't remember a time when she'd been so happy. Yes, she was deliriously happy, but she knew it couldn't last. She knew that at some point she was going to have to call a halt, before she got to the stage when the inevitable separation would be too traumatic.

'Everything OK, Jacky?'

She smiled up at Pierre, as she always did when the dark thoughts about the future threatened her present happiness.

'Everything's fine! I've finished the boring paperwork so now I can get on with some real work. How's everything out there in the reception area?'

'Still relatively quiet, thank goodness. I came in early so I could go and see Charles Lanvin.'

'How is he?' Jacky had become very fond of their patient, who had been transferred to the surgical ward since they'd first treated him in Urgences. 'I haven't seen him since his latest operation.'

'He's making excellent progress,' Pierre told her. 'It's been decided that his colostomy can be reversed soon.'

'I'm glad about that. He certainly wasn't happy with the thought that his colostomy bag might be permanent.

We were all hoping it would be temporary. And how's the bladder situation?'

'The repair of bladder has been successful. His urethral catheter was removed yesterday and he's passed urine.'

Jacky smiled. 'That's excellent. I saw him last week and he was telling me how thrilled he is that he's got full sensation in the lower half of his body now.'

'He's been so lucky! To be honest, I didn't expect the outcome of this case to be so good. The surgeons have done a brilliant job, and he's been a positive, determined patient.'

Pierre smiled. 'These are some of the perks of being a doctor, aren't they? Seeing a patient regaining their health against all the odds. Do you know, I felt positively inspired when I went back to my office to tackle the awful admin work. Then I went out to see what had turned up in Reception.'

'And what was happening there?'

'I sutured a leg, then discharged a patient who'd been admitted with a suspected coronary thrombosis that wasn't...'

'You discharged the patient?' Jacky moved across the room to fill the kettle and spoon coffee grounds into the cafetière. 'So what was the real diagnosis?'

Pierre walked over to the window and leaned against the sill as he watched Jacky.

'Excessive wind, to put it in layman's terms. Apparently, the man, an English tourist, ate an enormous curry last night. He was excessively overweight so I suggested he try to lose some weight when he goes back to England.'

He turned round to look out of the window. 'It's a good thing it's a quiet morning because a couple of those workmen are sitting on the ground, sunbathing in one of the ambulance bays, and the rest are so slow that… *Attend! Oh, mon Dieu…*'

'*Qu'est ce qu'il y a?* What's the matter?'

'An ambulance has just rammed into one of the men and there's another ambulance following closely behind. *On y va!* Let's go!'

Pierre flung open the door and they hurried down the corridor, out through the main door and across to where one of the porters, summoned from Reception, had just arrived with a trolley.

It was impossible to assess the injured man's condition as they carefully lifted their blood-covered patient onto the trolley.

'Let's get him inside, *tout de suite*!' Pierre said.

'Emergency here, Doctor,' called the driver of the second ambulance as he opened the back doors.

'The old beach café collapsed,' the driver continued, as one of the medics unloaded a patient. 'At least ten people injured. Another two ambulances are on their way here.'

'I'll deal with this patient,' Pierre said as they arrived back in reception with the injured workman. 'You'd better treat the patients from the beach café. Marie has just sent out a call for more help.'

Jacky's first patient was a six-year-old boy who was crying for his mother. 'She came in with me but they put her on another trolley. She's gone to sleep and I couldn't wake her up.'

Jacky quietly asked one of the nurses to make enquiries and report back. 'Grégoire, we'll find out where your *maman* is, as soon as possible. But now I want to check on how you are. If you could lie still on this couch for a little while…'

His right arm was obviously fractured, she deduced as she carefully avoided putting any pressure on the unnaturally aligned limb. But there was some bruising over the abdomen, which worried her. It could indicate some internal injury. She ordered an ultrasound scan for the abdomen and an X-ray for the arm.

During her examination she'd made a point of getting the boy to talk to her so that he would lose some of his fear. The nurse still hadn't returned with news of his mother. She didn't want him to relive the awful experience of being inside a building that had collapsed but that was all he wanted to talk about.

'I was having an ice cream,' he told her. 'We were sitting at a table on the front terrace of the old café. Have you been there? It's a real dump but the ice cream's good.'

'No, I haven't been there,' Jacky said, as she continued examining the little boy. 'I saw it when I walked along the beach one day.'

She didn't say that she'd heard it was to be pulled down soon. No doubt there would have to be a full inquiry into why it had remained open.

'The wind was blowing off the sea, I remember.' Grégoire was silent for a moment before he continued. 'And then a piece of wood fell down from the roof of the terrace and hit Maman on the head…and she went to sleep…'

Jacky took hold of the little boy's left hand, the one that wasn't injured. He looked up at her, his eyes wide and staring as he continued talking. 'I went round the table to tell Maman to wake up because we had to escape. All the roof was now falling in and the people were screaming and…and then something hit my arm and I fell down on the floor…'

'I've found Grégoire's mother,' the nurse told Jacky

quietly, as she hurried in through the door. 'She's unconscious. One of the neurological firm is on his way.'

'Thanks, Nurse.'

'What's happened to Maman?'

The small face was puckering up again and Grégoire's lower lip was trembling.

'Maman is still asleep, Grégoire. The doctor is going to do everything he can to make her better. Nurse is going to take you to X-Ray now so that they can take a picture of the bone in your arm.'

'It's broken, isn't it?'

'Yes, I think it is,' Jacky said gently. 'The X-ray picture will tell us exactly what's happened.'

'If I get one of those cast things on it, I'd like a blue one, *s'il vous plaît*. My friend at school had a brown one and I thought that was really boring.'

Jacky smiled down at the little boy who was trying so hard to be brave. 'You'll have to ask the plaster technician if there are any blue ones. If not, you'll be able to choose another colour.'

'But not brown.'

'No, not brown,' Jacky said solemnly.

It was so good to see a spark of life coming back into her patient's eyes. Whatever the outcome with his mother, he would survive. He had a plucky spirit. But she hoped that his mother's life wasn't in danger.

She worked through the day without a break. Two patients who had been in the middle of the café where the damage had been the worst had suffered multiple injuries and died soon after admission. Of the patients who survived, five had broken limbs, two required surgery for internal injuries and four had bruising and cuts, requiring sutures. Five people had made miraculous escapes.

*   *   *

As Jacky went back to her office at the end of the day, she kicked off her shoes and went straight over to the kettle she'd filled that morning. The automatic switch had worked, as she'd known it would. The unused coffee grounds were still sitting at the bottom of the cafetière. As she sank down into her favourite shabby armchair she wondered if Pierre would call in when he'd finished or if he'd go straight home.

As she was pouring the hot water onto the grounds the door opened. It was Pierre.

'I came to see if you'd made that coffee yet, Jacky.'

She smiled 'It's just ready now.'

He grinned as he flopped down into a chair. 'So what took you so long?'

'Oh, I had one or two little jobs to do. Other than that, nothing much happened today, did it?'

She handed him a cup of coffee, before removing her white coat and dumping it in the basket she reserved for laundry.

'I hadn't noticed the bloodstains while I was working,' she said, as she realised she'd been walking around wearing a most unsightly coat.

'You look fine now,' Pierre said fondly. 'I've got good news about your little patient, Grégoire. There are no internal injuries.'

'Thank goodness for that. He's a plucky little boy! What colour was the cast on his arm?'

'I think it was…yes, it was blue. Why?'

Jacky smiled. 'Good. That's what he wanted. These things can be really important when you're going through a rough time. Is there any news from the neurological firm about his mother?'

Pierre frowned. 'Cécile, his mother is still in a coma. We've transferred her to the preliminary medical ward.

The consultant neurologist is with her now, assessing her condition.'

Jacky leaned back in her armchair and closed her eyes. 'I hope and pray that…that she'll be all right.'

She felt Pierre's fingers closing around hers. She opened her eyes. The tender expression on his face was, oh, so comforting. She knew she shouldn't take things to heart when a patient was suffering, but she couldn't help identifying with the little boy.

'I hope Grégoire isn't going to lose his mother,' she said quietly. 'It's an awful thing for a child…'

She broke off, realising that Pierre's child was a motherless boy. She was treading on sensitive ground. 'I'm sorry, Pierre. I was thinking of myself. I—'

He squeezed her hand. 'I know you were. You've known what it's like to have to grow up too quickly. But…but, you see, Christophe never knew his mother. In some ways that makes it easier for him, but in others…'

He sighed and leaned back in his chair. 'Anyway. I've got a huge problem. Guy wants Nadine to go with him to Paris tomorrow for a couple of days. He's still got the cast on his leg so he can't drive. I'll have to let Nadine go.'

'Can't you arrange to take a couple of days off from Urgences? You're the boss.'

'Not tomorrow. I've got an important meeting in the morning which I can't miss. I've already scheduled myself off duty in the afternoon and the following day. But I've still got to phone the agency to arrange cover for the morning. Another stranger arriving in Christophe's life…'

'Poor little lamb.' Jacky hesitated. 'If you could rearrange my off duty and schedule me to have tomorrow off, I could look after Christophe.'

'Jacky, there's nothing I'd like better but…'

'But what?' She stood up and walked over to the window, staring out into the darkening forecourt. The lights had just been switched on, revealing that the repairs to the tarmac were still unfinished. Not surprising, considering the day's activities. She was still waiting for Pierre to answer her. She knew what the problem was. Better change the subject. She'd offered her help. There was nothing more she could do.

'How's the injured workman who was struck by the ambulance?' she asked, turning round.

Pierre stood up and joined her by the window. 'He's still in Theatre. He's suffered multiple injuries, poor man. One leg has been amputated. The orthopaedic consultant is working on the other leg at the moment. He's going to try and save it but…'

He broke off, looking down at Jacky and taking hold of her by the shoulders. 'Compared to the suffering of our patients today, my problems are very small, aren't they? Marcel and Debbie helped me out during the school holidays when Nadine had time off, but they're at their holiday cottage on the coast near Bordeaux now…'

She took a deep breath. 'Pierre, I would love to take care of Christophe tomorrow. We got on so well when I first met him. I'd really like to see him again…'

'And he'd like to see you,' Pierre said. 'He's always asking when you're going to come to the house again, but…' His voice trailed away.

Jacky was silent as she looked at Pierre. 'You're being very stubborn about this.'

'I'm not being stubborn! I simply don't want him to get hurt if…when…'

She swallowed hard. 'When we split up?'

He drew her against him. 'I don't want it to happen. But I have this recurring nightmare. It came again last night. Liliane is in labour, calling for me…and I'm not there.'

He took a deep breath. 'I wasn't at the birth you know. I wasn't there when she died. That was unforgivable, wasn't it?'

'Everything is forgivable,' she said. 'There must have been a valid reason why you couldn't be there. Why weren't you there, Pierre?'

'I was speaking at a medical conference. I had to switch off my mobile because I was in the lecture theatre. Liliane was at our apartment in Paris. She was only seven months pregnant and in apparent good health. I had no qualms about leaving her…at the time…'

Jacky waited. Pierre stared down at her with a haunted expression as if reliving the events of that fateful day.

'Her obstetrician hadn't detected the abnormality in her uterus that was to prove fatal.'

He broke off. Jacky remained quiet, waiting for him to continue. She wanted to reach out to him…to comfort him. But why did she feel he was withholding something?

'As far as I can gather, from all the medical reports that were given to me afterwards, she must have woken up feeling ill that morning. She couldn't have known she was in labour or… Well, anyway, she'd started bleeding. She tried to make a call for an ambulance but she must have fainted before she could give her address.'

He swallowed hard. 'By the time the ambulance managed to track her down and break into the apartment, Liliane had given birth and was bleeding profusely. The paramedics found her lying on the bathroom floor, unconscious. Baby Christophe was lying between her legs, barely alive. Liliane died on the way to hospital…'

Jacky cradled Pierre in her arms as he lowered his head to her shoulder. She murmured words of comfort in

French, but she didn't feel she was reaching him. Pierre was never going to be able to forget. How could he ever forget something so traumatic?

Unless someone enlightened him about… No, it would be even worse if Marcel told Pierre his wife had been unfaithful! Pierre must be allowed to hang on to the memories he cherished of the happy marriage he'd shared with Liliane before she'd been so traumatically taken from him. Nobody should be allowed to disillusion him.

'It's incredible that Christophe survived,' Jacky said gently.

He sighed. 'The paramedics were brilliant. They had an incubator in the ambulance and they did everything they could to ensure he survived…as he did. But, then, he's a real fighter!'

'Like his father,' she said as she moved away.

Jacky was afraid she might start crying. Pierre's revelations had been deeply disturbing. And too many of her own traumatic memories had been stirred up.

He came up behind her and put his arms around her waist. 'Jacky, it's good of you to offer to look after Christophe tomorrow.' He hesitated. 'Can I take you up on that?'

She swung round. 'Of course!' She smiled as she felt her spirits lifting again. 'But you'll have to check with the boss of Urgences as to whether my off-duty can be changed. I've heard he's impossibly stubborn.'

'Not always.' He drew in his breath. He'd just made a big decision. 'So, would you like to come round for breakfast tomorrow?'

As she walked along the road towards Pierre's house next morning she was wondering what it was that had made him change his mind. Something cathartic had happened between them when he'd told her about his wife's tragic death. It was as if he'd undergone a change of heart when he'd confided in her. Whatever it was, she was relieved. Because she was so looking forward to seeing Christophe again.

She turned into his drive, her feet crunching over the gravel. She paused to remove a small stone from her sandals. Flat sandals, easy to get on and off, were de rigueur today because she intended to take Christophe to the beach. She had a bag with her swimwear, a large bottle of mineral water and some biscuits. If they needed anything else, she would take Christophe to one of the beach cafés.

Pierre threw open the door and Christophe rushed out to meet her. '*Bonjour*, Jacky.'

Christophe raised his little face for the customary greeting that all French children learned from an early age. Jacky knelt down so that they were the same height as they kissed on both cheeks.

'Jacky, *le petit déjeuner est prêt*. We were waiting for breakfast until you arrived.'

He was pulling her by the hand so that they could get on with breakfast. She smiled up at Pierre as she passed him in the doorway. They exchanged greetings and kisses, but Christophe was hungry and didn't want to wait any longer. Impatiently, the little boy tugged at her hand.

The delicious aroma of freshly baked croissants met her as she followed Christophe into the kitchen. 'Mmm, I love croissants.'

'*Moi aussi*, so do I,' Christophe said, settling himself on his chair before reaching for the apricot conserve. 'The top of this jar is so… *C'est si difficile*. Jacky, *je pense que—*'

The top flew off before Jacky could reach forward t<

help him. '*Pas de probleme. Ce n'est pas important,*' she reassured the little boy, as she spooned up the spilt jam from the tablecloth.

'I knew I shouldn't have shown off by laying the kitchen table with a tablecloth,' Pierre said with a wry grin as he leaned over Jacky with a damp cloth and began scrubbing at the stain.

He moved back and sat down on his chair. 'That will be OK for now. I got carried away this morning when I knew I was expecting a VIP guest.'

'*Parle français, Papa, s'il te plaît!* Speak French to me. What is a VIP guest?'

'It's somebody very important,' Pierre said, passing the basket of croissants across the table to Jacky.

'Is Jacky very important?'

Pierre smiled. 'She is to me.'

'And me,' Christophe piped up. 'Because she's going to look after me today. What shall we do, Jacky? Do you like playing football in the garden?'

'Why don't we take the football to the beach?'

'*Fantastique!* And then we can swim. I can swim properly…well, I still wear armbands in the sea. Papa says a big wave might carry me away because I'm small and I can only do a few strokes before I have to stop…'

Jacky looked across the table as Christophe munched and chattered happily. Her eyes locked with Pierre's. At that moment she could feel the most wonderful rapport between them. He reached across the table and felt for her hand.

'Sorry my hand is so sticky with Christophe's jam,' she whispered in English as his fingers closed around hers.

'Doesn't matter. So is mine. We'll simply stick together.'

She smiled, enjoying the current of sensual feeling running between them. It felt so good to be accepted into this warm family. There would be problems ahead but for the moment she was living one day at a time.

Pierre kissed her as he left for the hospital. 'Keep your mobile switched on while you're at the beach, Jacky.'

'I thought you were going to be in an important meeting this morning.'

'I am. The board of governors are not the easiest people to deal with. I've got to persuade them to part with some more cash for our department. Wish me luck. I'll be switched off while I'm in there, but I'm theoretically off duty after the meeting. If I can get away in time I'll come out to meet you at the beach.'

'That would be nice.'

A little voice was calling to her from upstairs. 'Jacky! Jacky, I can't find my swimming stuff. *Tu peux m'aider?* Can you help me?'

'*J'arrive tout de suite*, Christophe,' she called back.

Pierre smiled as he stepped out of the house on to the drive. 'Nadine puts all Christophe's clothes in that chest of drawers in his room. Try the top drawer. He can't reach up to see what's in there.'

'OK. Will do.' She gave a final wave as he drove out of the drive before closing the door.

'I'm coming, Christophe,' she called, as she ran up the stairs.

CHAPTER EIGHT

As THEY walked along the beach, Christophe ran ahead, kicking the football. Occasionally, he would turn and kick the football towards her and she made a valiant effort to return it. Her sandals weren't ideal for the job! As she flipped them off and carried them in her hand she realised that she hadn't felt so completely at peace with herself in a long time.

Yes, she loved little Christophe. If things had been different she would have been playing on the beach with her own child.

'Christophe, shall we stop here and have a swim?' she called.

Christophe picked up the football and scampered back to her across the sand. 'Can you swim, Jacky?'

'Yes, I love swimming. Come on, we'll go up near the sand dunes and get changed there.'

She wrapped her towel around her, wriggling out of her clothes into her bikini. Christophe had stripped off and was struggling into his swimming trunks.

'There! I'm ready, Jacky!'

He held out his hand towards her and together they ran down the sand into the sea.

'It's cold! Why is the sea cold when the sand is so warm, Jacky?'

'The sea is very big. It takes a long time to heat up even when the weather is hot.'

'So even if we brought down a big bucket of hot water, it wouldn't make much difference, would it?' Christophe asked, putting his little hand in hers and looking up at her with a beguiling expression.

'No, it wouldn't,' she said solemnly.

'Let me show you how I can swim now.'

'Wait a moment. One of your armbands is slipping off.' She adjusted the bands to make sure they were firm. 'OK. You can swim now.'

Christophe threw himself into the knee-high water and did several strokes of doggy paddle before a wave slipped over him. He came up, spluttering and swallowing water, but still smiling. 'I'm going to do some more.'

After several attempts Christophe was making headway. 'Jacky, swim beside me.'

The water was too shallow for her to swim and she didn't want to take Christophe out of his depth, but she managed to do a gentle glide, which pleased him.

'We're swimming together, aren't we? Like the dolphins do. Have you ever seen a dolphin, Jacky?'

'I've never seen one along this coast. But further south…'

As she launched into an account of all the dolphins she'd ever seen, Christophe listened, fascinated. He told her he wanted to travel because he wanted to see tigers and lions and…

The list of the creatures the little boy was interested in was endless. They splashed and talked, swam a little, having a great time. As they ran back up the beach to towel themselves dry, Jacky was thinking what a sensitive, intelligent child Christophe was.

In spite of not having a mother to help him, he'd developed into a delightful little boy. But, then, he had a loving, caring father. She sighed inwardly as she stretched out on the sand in a dry bikini. Christophe had begun to dig a castle in the sand. Jacky had brought the small plastic spade she'd found amongst his toys.

Her mobile rang. She reached for her bag.

'Pierre! I thought you would still be in your meeting.'

'The meeting finished early. Most unexpected! It was a piece of cake, as you say in England! I soon brought them round to my way of thinking and they've granted the extra money for us. I'd expected it would take me all morning to persuade them.'

'But that's wonderful!'

'So I'm coming along to join you now.'

'Is that Papa?' Christophe asked eagerly.

Jacky smiled. 'Christophe would like to speak to you, Pierre.'

'Put him on, Jacky.'

Christophe smiled happily as he chatted to his father. 'Yes, I'm building a big castle. Can you come and help me to—? Oh, *magnifique! Tout de suite! Oui, Papa*!'

The little boy handed the phone back to Jacky. *'Papa veut parler avec toi, Jacky.'*

'Where exactly are you, Jacky?'

Jacky gave Pierre clear directions and he promised to join them in a few minutes.

Christophe was already digging in the sand again.

'I'm coming to help you with your castle,' she called.

'Bien! Can you find some more of these pebbles, Jacky? I want to put them on the roof when the castle is big enough.'

Time had begun to mean nothing to her as she searched for stones and Christophe added sand to his castle.

Her heart leapt for joy when she heard the sound of Pierre's voice. He was running through the soft sand at the edge of the dunes, carrying a huge plastic bag in one hand. She saw he'd changed into jeans and a short-sleeved polo shirt. He looked young and boyish again, just like he had in those far-off days before his life had been beset with problems.

'Papa! Papa!' Christophe hurled himself on his father.

'I bought a couple of new spades from the shop by the car park.'

'Wow! They're much bigger than my old one,' Christophe said, pulling out a huge spade from the plastic bag. *'Merci beaucoup, Papa.'*

Pierre looked over his son's head at Jacky. 'Are you OK?'

She smiled. 'Never better! We're having a lovely time.'

'I can see that.' He reached out and clasped her hand. She revelled in the touch of his skin against hers.

'Papa. We need to get on with the castle,' Christophe said, tugging at Pierre's other hand.

'OK, I'm ready for action,' Pierre said as he moved over to the pile of sand. 'We need to flatten the sides of the walls with our spades like this, Christophe.'

'Do you think we need any more stones for the roof, Christophe?' Jacky asked.

'I think we've got enough now, don't you, Papa?'

'Enough for two castles! Did you gather all those beautiful stones, Jacky?'

'I certainly did. I'll start to decorate this section here if you'll flatten the top for me, Christophe. *Merci beaucoup.*'

'Jacky, where did you learn how to decorate sand castles?' Christophe asked, leaning on his new spade to watch the patterns she was making.

'I lived by the sea when I was a little girl,' she said, as she fixed a pretty grey and white pebble in place.

'By this sea, here?'

'Yes, but further down the coast.'

'Did your *maman* and *papa* help you with your sand castles like you're doing with me?'

'Well…no. My parents didn't like the beach very much, so I went by myself or with my friends.'

She was very much aware that Pierre had stopped digging and was listening.

'I lived near the same beach when I was a boy,' he told Christophe.

'*Vraiment!* Really!' Christophe laid his spade on the sand, sitting back on his heels as he stared at them in amazement. 'So did you play together?'

Jacky smiled. 'Not really. Your *papa* was older than me and he didn't want to play with a little girl. He liked to play football with his big friends.'

'Yes, but sometimes we met on the beach,' Pierre said, his voice full of nostalgic warmth. 'Like the time you slipped on the rocks.'

She moved nearer so that she was midway between Pierre and Christophe. 'And you carried me all the way to your father's surgery so he could suture my leg. I remember that day so vividly.'

Pierre put one finger under her chin and raised her eyes towards his. 'But you were very young.'

'Yes, I was very young…but I still remember it,' she said breathily.

Their eyes locked and the feeling of mutual admiration was palpable.

Christophe sensed the love flowing between his father and Jacky as he moved closer so that he was enclosed in a tiny space between them in what seemed to him like a family cuddle.

Jacky could feel the emotional vibes running between the three of them. She drew in her breath to savour the precious moment before she moved away and began looking through the pile of stones.

'Will you put that big white stone on here, Jacky?' Christophe said.

They were all back on track, working together on the castle, but the warm bond that had just been sealed between the three of them remained.

At the end of the morning, when they all agreed there was nothing more to be done to improve their perfect castle, Pierre announced that it was time for lunch.

'There's a little café a short way from here. Marcel told me about it. He and Debbie often go there and they've told me the lunch is very good.'

Jacky dusted the sand off Christophe and herself before putting on her linen trousers and crinkly cotton top.

'I found a good place to park the car nearby,' Pierre said. 'We can walk to the café from here.'

'I'm afraid Christophe's T-shirt is stained with chocolate ice cream,' Jacky said. 'We got some as we walked along the sand.'

Pierre smiled. 'He looks fine, Jacky. He's happy, that's the main thing.'

He leaned forward and kissed her cheek. A simple gesture but Jacky felt a delicious frisson as Pierre's lips touched her skin.

'I'll put our things in the car,' he told her as he moved away.

Five minutes later he was back. Christophe ran along ahead of them as they walked towards the place where they were going to have lunch.

'So, you didn't have any problems with Christophe while I was at the hospital?' Pierre glanced sideways at Jacky, thinking how calm and relaxed she looked.

'No problems at all,' she said. 'We had a great time

together. He's a very intelligent little boy. We discussed all sorts of subjects—animals, birds, books he likes you or Nadine to read to him at bedtime. Books he's beginning to read himself…'

Pierre reached for her hand. 'That's how he likes to be treated. Some of the people who've cared for him have talked down to him, sometimes haven't recognised that his refusal to do what they wanted him to do was simply a cry for help. And that's when the tantrums used to start.'

'I honestly can't imagine Christophe being difficult,' she said. 'It's such a pity—'

She broke off. She'd been going to say something about continuity of care with the same person, but that would only bring up the insoluble problem that she didn't like to think about. She was well aware that Christophe had already bonded with her and she with him.

Pierre cleared his throat. 'You were going to say?'

'I was going to say, is that the café over there in the wide dip in the dunes?' she said quickly.

'No, you weren't,' he said quietly. 'It worries me that there have been so many changes in Christophe's life but…' He drew in his breath. 'But let's not discuss it now while we're having such a great time. The sun is shining, we've got the rest of the day together. Come on, let's head Christophe in the right direction. He looks as if he's making for the sea now.'

They received a warm welcome from the owners of the small restaurant. Henri, a rotund, middle-aged man, met them as they walked in through the door and his wife, Antoinette, came out of the kitchen, dusting down her floury hands on her apron.

Jacky gathered from the conversation that Pierre had phoned ahead to reserve a table and had mentioned that they were friends of Marcel and Debbie. The dining room was small and every table was occupied except the table by the window which Henri had reserved for them.

Antoinette spent a lot of time with young Christophe, insisting that she give him a glass of her freshly squeezed orange juice. She produced cushions for his chair to make it higher before placing the orange juice in front of him.

'*Un petit apéritif pour vous, madame?*' Henri enquired.

Jacky said she would like her favourite kir. Pierre decided on a glass of pastis with water.

They ate a starter course of *pâté maison*, which Antoinette said she'd made herself. Christophe ate all his starter and main course, together with some bread, but managed to chatter continually throughout the meal.

Jacky put down her fork and dipped her fingers in the finger bowl. Their main course of lemon sole had been delicious.

'Sometimes I don't like fish,' Christophe said, as he swallowed the final piece from his plate. 'But this was really good. Not at all smelly. Sometimes the fish we have to eat at school at lunchtime smells bad and then I leave it all on the side of my plate.'

Jacky leaned forward. 'But don't you feel hungry during the afternoon?'

'*Bien sûr!* Of course, but…'

The little boy gave a Gallic shrug. Jacky thought how much he resembled his father when he made that typically French gesture.

Antoinette came out of the kitchen to ask Christophe if he would prefer ice cream or apple pie for his dessert. He chose ice cream.

'*Citron, vanille, chocolat ou fraise?*' Antoinette enquired.

Christophe was taking a long time to decide which flavour he wanted. In the end, Antoinette solved the problem by giving him a plate with four small helpings of lemon, vanilla, chocolate and strawberry.

'*Votre fils est adorable!*' Antoinette said, placing her hand on Jacky's arm.

Jacky was about to correct Antoinette's assumption that she was Christophe's mother when Pierre cut in quickly. '*Merci, madame.* We are very proud of him.'

Jacky took a sip of her coffee. Both she and Pierre had decided against having dessert. She looked across the table at Pierre. He met her gaze with an enigmatic expression. Now was not the right time to question why he hadn't put Antoinette wise about their relationship. Was it possible he was indulging in daydreams, as she was?

She smiled at him across the table and he returned her smile with that laconic expression on his handsome face that had the instant effect of reigniting her desires. She would have liked to go for a long siesta somewhere…her place…his place… What did it matter? So long as they could be together, making love for the whole afternoon.

She suppressed a shiver of desire as she gazed at him. She could tell from the way he parted his lips, his tongue briefly skimming the lower one, that he was thinking along the same lines as she was.

Christophe reached across the table and took hold of Pierre's sleeve. 'Can we go back to that place on the beach where I made my sand castle, Papa? You could help me make another one at the side of it, couldn't you?'

'Of course I will,' Pierre said.

His wordless conversation with Jacky was over. He touched her arm as he pulled back her chair. She stood up and turned round to kiss him lightly on the cheek.

'That wasn't too inappropriate, was it?' she whispered.

He put a hand on her waist. 'We're allowed a little display of affection even in a restaurant.'

He was looking down at her with such a wistful expression that she thought her knees would start to buckle beneath her.

'Do you have any plans for this evening?' he whispered.

'I'll have to check in my diary.'

'Why are you whispering?' Christophe said, sliding down from his chair and coming round the table to join them.

'We're planning what to do this afternoon.' Pierre smiled at his son. 'Come on, let's go back to the beach and make an even bigger castle this time.'

Christophe gave a happy laugh as he linked hands with Pierre and Jacky. '*Oui*, and then we can swim again and play with my football and...'

At the end of the afternoon, Jacky felt exhilarated. Both she and Pierre had thrown themselves into playing with Christophe. Consequently, the little boy's happiness and exuberance had rubbed off on them.

Her thoughts turned to the evening. She suppressed a shiver, knowing that when Christophe was fast asleep she and Pierre would be free to indulge themselves...to pamper each other...to make love...

It would seem even more romantic because they'd had to contain their feelings and wait until they were alone.

'You're very quiet, Jacky,' Pierre said as he helped her pile the things in the car. 'What's on your mind?'

She glanced down at Christophe, who was transferring pebbles from his bucket to a large plastic bag.

'I'll tell you later,' she said quietly.

Pierre smiled. 'Ah, I think I can guess. At least, I hope I can.'

He touched her arm and something akin to an electric current of desire ran through her body. She must suppress her feelings a little longer…

Jacky spent a lot of time that evening with Christophe, sitting out on the terrace, reading to him and watching him painting a picture with the new paints that Pierre had bought him recently.

Pierre prepared an omelette. Jacky tossed a salad and they sat at the kitchen table. When they'd finished, Pierre refilled Jacky's wineglass and leaned back against his chair.

'It's been a long day,' Pierre said, as he watched Christophe trying hard to stay awake. 'Are you tired, Christophe?'

'No. Well a bit…Jacky will you take me up to bed?'

'Of course. I'd love to.' She stood up.

'I'll clear up the kitchen,' Pierre said.

The preparations for bed took a long time but Jacky and Christophe were enjoying themselves. As Christophe lay in the bath he showed Jacky all his plastic water toys.

'You've got so many I'm surprised there's room for you in the bath,' she said.

Pierre came into the bathroom, watching the happy scene with a tender expression on his face.

'Everything OK, Jacky?' he said, his voice husky.

She was kneeling on the floor, her face flushed and steamy from the hot water in the bath. She looked up and smiled.

'Everything's fine.'

He gave her a rakish grin. 'Not too tired?'

He was making it patently obvious why he was enquiring! 'I'm never too tired.'

'Good.' Pierre reached down to where she was crouched beside the bath and caressed the back of her hair, his hands briefly moving to the nape of her neck.

'I'll finish off in the kitchen,' he said. 'Looks like you might be in here quite a while.'

'I don't want to hurry things,' Jacky said.

'Quite right.' He turned at the door and blew her a kiss.

Later, as Jacky placed a cool sheet over Christophe and said goodnight, Pierre came into his son's bedroom.

'I've changed his duvet for a sheet,' she said. 'The duvet was too hot.'

He put a hand on her waist as he leaned down to kiss his little boy.

'Goodnight, Christophe. Sleep well. I love you.'

Christophe's eyes were closing. 'Goodnight, Papa. I love you. Goodnight, Jacky. I love you.'

She felt Pierre's hand tighten on her waist. 'And I love you, too, Christophe,' she said.

It was a simple, truthful thing to say but, oh, it was so poignant for her.

It was as if she'd been given back her own son. For a second her heart seemed to stop. How could she ever walk away from this little boy—and from this wonderful man?

Pierre's hand tightened on her waist and he drew her against him. Christophe was still asleep. Gently he led her away from the slumbering child's bed.

As he closed the door in his bedroom he took her into his arms. His kiss was full of longing for her.

The night stretching ahead belonged only to them...

* * *

'Jacky, why are you leaving?' In the early dawn light, Pierre tried to focus his eyes on the bedside clock. 'I've got the whole day off. It's much too early to—'

'I have to go,' Jacky said firmly as she buttoned up her crinkly shirt. 'I'm on duty this morning.'

'Jacky, I'll phone in and arrange cover for you today. I can rearrange the schedule. It won't be a problem.'

He leapt out of bed, shrugging into his robe and hurrying round the bed.

'No, I need to get back,' she said quietly. 'Christophe will enjoy having you all to himself today.'

He put his hands on the side of her arms, holding her, his eyes quizzical.

'But what's happened? We've had such a wonderful time together.' He drew her against him and she didn't resist. 'Why do you have to rush away?'

She looked up into his eyes and felt her treacherous body responding. No, her mind was made up. She'd lain awake after they'd made love in the night. She'd been so happy, but she'd known it was an ephemeral happiness. It couldn't last. And she was becoming too complacent about it. Her heart would break when their relationship ended.

Separation was inevitable sooner or later. She'd decided she would go on seeing Pierre but she had to keep a hold on her emotions. Another day with Pierre and Christophe, pretending they were a real family, was out of the question. It wasn't fair on Christophe. She was worried about the effect she was having on him. How could a little boy of five understand that nothing lasted for ever?

Pierre drew in his breath. 'You've got that worried look on your face. Can't we simply live for the moment…not think too far ahead? Jacky, I've never been so happy!'

She looked up at him. 'Nor have I,' she whispered. 'But I need to get back to the real world for a while.' She smiled. 'Look, it's not as if I'm leaving you for ever! I simply think we've spent enough time together as a...as a...'

'As a family?' he said quietly.

She nodded.

He swallowed hard. 'I see your point. I've been the one who insisted we didn't involve Christophe in our relationship. But he's involved now.'

'Yes, he is. And some time in the future Christophe will have to realise that...'

'Jacky, we'll face that problem together when it comes.'

'Will we?' She took a deep breath. 'Look, I must leave now.'

'If that's what you've decided,' he said in a resigned tone. Lowering his head, he kissed her lightly on the mouth.

She pulled away and made for the door, the rational part of her brain telling her it was the right thing to do, her heart telling her to stay longer.

But the longer she committed herself wholeheartedly to Pierre and Christophe, the harder it was going to be for all of them when the inevitable split came. There was no solution as far as she could see. So she had to keep a small part of herself uncommitted and rational.

CHAPTER NINE

FOR the next couple of weeks Jacky felt as if she was treading on eggshells as far as Pierre was concerned. He hadn't referred to their conversation at the end of the last night they'd spent together, but she could tell it was on his mind.

She'd instinctively tried to cool it, to distance herself from the problems in their relationship. But whenever she was working with Pierre at the hospital—like this morning—she could feel the tension growing between them.

She fixed the X-rays she was holding on the lighted screen in the treatment room and scanned them carefully. Beside her, Pierre frowned as he surveyed the X-rays of their patient's injured leg.

He'd only just returned from the main reception area, having been called away to another patient, so Jacky had been in charge of Gaston, their car-crash victim. She'd asked for the fractured leg and foot to be X-rayed from every angle and Pierre could see that extensive surgery would be needed.

He leaned forward and pointed to the X-ray he was studying. 'Fragments of bone are missing where the foot was badly injured and ruptured spontaneously. They're probably somewhere on the road where the car crash occurred. Anyway, the bone fragments would no longer be viable. The paramedics told me that the engine broke through into the passenger footwell and smashed into Gaston's foot.'

Pierre turned round to glance at their twenty-year-old

patient, stretched out on the examination couch. He'd sedated him as soon as he'd arrived and, mercifully, he was still asleep.

Jacky was studying the X-rays of the leg. 'The tibia and fibula are fractured in several places...look, here...and here,' she pointed out to Pierre.

He nodded as he turned his attention to the upper part of the leg. 'The femur appears intact. That's a relief. We may still be able to save the whole leg and possibly the foot. I've alerted the orthopaedic firm. They're going to fit Gaston into their operating schedule later this morning. The operation will take several hours but they're prepared to work in shifts if necessary.'

Marie came into the treatment room. 'Why don't you two take a break for a few minutes? Everything's under control out there at the moment, but we're sure to need you later on. Don't worry. I'll get your patient ready for Theatre. Orthopaedics have just contacted me to say they'll operate on him in one hour.'

'Thanks, Marie,' Pierre said. 'We'll take you up on that.'

'Do you think Marie is trying to matchmake by sending us off together?' Pierre said lightly, as they walked along the corridor that led to Jacky's office.

Jacky laughed. 'I doubt it.'

'Do you know, that's the first time I've heard you laugh since...well, for ages,' he finished off hurriedly.

'You mean since I left early from your bedroom, when you didn't want me to go, don't you?' Jacky said, as she opened the door of her office.

Pierre waited until they were inside before drawing her against him. He closed the door behind them and his arms tightened around her.

She looked up at him, her heart thudding, her emotions

churning. 'Yes, I suppose it is the first time I've laughed,' she said.

'And this is the first time you've allowed me to touch you since you left me that morning,' he said huskily.

'You haven't tried to touch me,' she said, as she looked up at him and tried to calm her churning emotions.

He raised an eyebrow. 'And can you blame me? You've been playing little Miss Ice Queen for two weeks. I didn't dare to come near you.'

'Little Miss Ice Queen! That's an interesting expression. Where did you pick that up?'

'Probably Australia. What does it matter? It suited you very well. You were unapproachable, Jacky.'

'I was trying to play it cool, if you must know,' she said, in a pseudo-haughty voice.

'And failing miserably! You're so transparent.' He lowered his voice to a mere whisper. 'But I love you, Jacky.'

She stared at him, her heart fluttering. He'd never said that before. She'd longed for him to say it, and now he actually had she couldn't believe it! And in English, too.

Maybe her cooling-off period had been no bad thing…except Pierre saying he loved her only added to her problems. She knew she couldn't commit herself to Pierre while he still worshipped his late wife. And even if he stopped worshipping her, she couldn't go along with a permanent relationship.

It wouldn't be fair to commit herself to Pierre when she couldn't give him more children. If the scales fell from his eyes concerning Liliane, he would need a woman who could give him the real family life he deserved.

'I've never told you I loved you before,' he whispered, his arms tightening around her. 'But in the last two weeks, when I thought I might have lost you, I did some thinking.'

She held her breath. 'And?'

'I've been thinking a great deal about where you and I are going and—'

'I've also been doing some thinking,' she broke in quickly. 'I'm not going to look too far ahead. I love being with you, Pierre, but…'

'But you don't love me?'

'Oh, but I do love you!' She clapped a hand over her mouth.

He drew her into his arms. 'You didn't mean to say that, did you?'

'There are simply too many insoluble problems,' she said. 'It's true that I love you…but there's no way that…'

The phone on her desk started ringing. She moved away and picked it up. 'Yes, Marie?'

Her spirits lifted as she listened. 'But that's wonderful! We'll come along now.'

She put the phone down.

'What's happened, Jacky?'

'Cécile, who's been in a coma since she was hit by a falling rafter in the beach café tragedy, has regained consciousness. Her little boy, Grégoire, and his father are on their way to see her. Grégoire has asked if it's possible for the two doctors who looked after him when he was admitted to come and meet him at his mother's bedside.'

'Of course we'll be there,' Pierre said, holding open the door for Jacky. 'I've been in to see Cécile many times since she was admitted. The neurological firm didn't hold out much hope, but miracles sometimes happen, don't they?'

Jacky lengthened her stride to keep up with Pierre. 'They certainly do. Remember Dominic, our little patient who was virtually dead after he'd been stuck at the bottom of the sea?'

'How could I forget?'

Jacky vividly remembered that morning in June, the first time she'd seen Pierre since she was sixteen. What an impact he'd made on her that day!

It had been a miracle that the child had survived, she thought as she followed Pierre into the medical ward.

Six-year-old Grégoire was sitting beside his mother's bed. He jumped up when Jacky and Pierre went in.

'*Regardez Maman!*' he said, pointing at his mother lying propped up against the pillows.

The patient lifted a hand from the sheet and attempted to smile. Her husband took hold of her hand and told her, gently, to save her strength.

Pierre moved to the bedside and spoke quietly to Cécile, telling her how pleased he was to see that she was recovering. But he advised her to rest quietly and said that he wasn't going to stay very long. The neurological consultant was coming to see her shortly and would want to assess her condition and explain the treatment he was going to arrange for her.

Cécile managed a wan smile. 'You have all been so good to me,' she said in a barely audible voice. 'For some time…I don't know how long…I knew you were here…but…but it was as if I was in a dream. People kept coming into my room but I didn't know how to…to open my eyes…how to speak…'

Grégoire leaned forward and kissed his mother's cheek. 'You're going to be fine, Maman,' he said happily. 'I didn't think you would ever wake up.'

A tear ran down Cécile's cheek. 'I wanted to tell you I could hear what you were saying but I didn't know how to break out of my dream.'

Cécile looked up at Jacky, a puzzled expression on her

face. 'I remember you were here sometimes, *Madame*. Are you a doctor?'

Jacky smiled. 'I was here when you were first brought into hospital.'

'I don't remember being brought in. I don't remember anything until…probably a few days ago…when I started coming round from my dream. I don't know where I've been but I'm glad to be back.'

Grégoire followed Jacky and Pierre to the door of the ward as they went out.

'How's your arm, Grégoire?' Jacky asked.

The young boy grinned happily. 'Look…no cast! It's better now. I wanted to keep the cast on to show my friends when I go back to school in September. The plaster man let me keep it, though. I'll take it with me.'

'The blue one?' Jacky said.

Grégoire laughed. 'How did you know it was blue?'

'I told Jacky I'd seen it,' Pierre said. 'I thought it was very smart.'

'So did I. I've hung it on the wall in my bedroom.'

'Grégoire!' called a feeble voice from inside the room.

'Better go back inside,' the boy said importantly. 'Maman needs me.'

'He's such a sweet little boy,' Jacky said as they walked back to her room. 'Do you think we've still got time for that coffee?'

Pierre pushed open the door. 'Marie knows where we are. She'll get in touch when we're needed.'

She switched on the kettle and reached for the cafetière. Pierre came over to fill their cups when the coffee was ready.

Jacky leaned back in her chair as she drank her coffee. 'In some ways it's seemed like a long hot summer but in others it's simply flown by. Everybody coming back from holiday and—'

'Talking of which…sorry to interrupt…I meant to ask you last week but you were in your unapproachable phase and I didn't dare. Marcel phoned up from Bordeaux to say that Debbie wants to fix a date to have us round for supper when they get back. Some time during the first week in September.'

'That's next week.'

'I know,' he said, with a sheepish grin. 'I was supposed to let Debbie know. She phoned again yesterday and left a message on my answering-machine. Can't think why it's so important we should get together as soon as they get back.'

Jacky had a distinct feeling that she knew why! Oh, dear! She hoped there wasn't going to be a confrontation between Marcel and Pierre. Supposing Marcel was about to tell the truth concerning Liliane. She hoped that Marcel wasn't planning to disillusion his friend and colleague. It would break Pierre's heart.

She suppressed a groan. She must speak to Debbie just in case.

'Everything OK?' Pierre looked puzzled. 'I thought you and Debbie were great friends. You're always going round to see her.'

'Yes, we are great friends,' she said quickly. 'I'd love to go for supper. I'll check my diary and give you a date.'

'Come on, Jacky. You haven't got that many social engagements, have you? I need to phone Debbie soon…like yesterday. You're off duty on Wednesday afternoon next week, aren't you?'

'If you say so. You made the duty roster.'

'So Wednesday evening would be OK, wouldn't it?'

She smiled, even though she couldn't help feeling apprehensive. 'Wednesday would be as good a day as any other.'

'Well, don't sound too excited about it, will you? It's only a simple supper with friends.'

If Marcel decided to reveal some unpleasant truths to Pierre it would be anything but a simple supper, she thought as she reached for the ringing phone on her desk. *'Nous arrivons, tout de suite, Marie…'*

On the day she was due to have supper with Debbie, Jacky phoned and left a message on the answering-machine to say she would arrive early. Pierre would come along later. In a way she was glad that Debbie wasn't around to take her call. It meant that she needn't have to explain why she going early.

As she walked along the road that led to Debbie's house she could feel her apprehension building up. She tried to stop herself worrying by looking at her surroundings.

Debbie's house was near the beginning of this road of beautiful, individually designed houses. *'Chemin de directeurs'* a junior doctor had jokingly called the road one day at the hospital. 'Consultants' road', that would be in English. It was certainly the sort of road that estate agents would describe as 'desirable' or 'much sought after'. Views over the sea, large gardens…the houses had everything.

She put a hand to her eyes to shield them from the dying rays of the early evening sun as she looked along the road as far as she could see. Pierre's house was hidden by the large trees at the edge of the property.

Thinking of Pierre made her worries return. When she'd last seen him he had been busy with a patient in the treatment room. He'd given her permission to leave early today, even though she hadn't given him any reason why she was going to arrive before he did.

She slowed her footsteps. She was here now. She took a deep breath as she walked along the drive, climbed the wide stone steps and rang the doorbell.

Debbie opened the door. 'Come in. I got your message.'

'It's lovely to see you back, Debbie,' Jacky said as she stepped inside the hall. 'How was the holiday?'

Debbie hugged her. 'The holiday was great, but it's always nice to be home. And it's good to see our friends again. We've missed you and Pierre so much. Come through into the sitting room where we can relax.'

Jacky sank down into one of the squashy armchairs and looked across the expanse of carpet towards her friend.

Debbie smiled. 'It's nice of you to come early, but why didn't you want to come later with Pierre?'

'I thought I might be able to help.'

'No, you didn't. You know perfectly well that Françoise doesn't even want me in the kitchen when she's cooking dinner for guests.' Debbie paused. 'Come clean, Jacky. What's on your mind?'

Jacky hesitated as she crossed then uncrossed her legs. 'Can't you guess?'

'Of course I can! I just wanted to hear it from you. You think I might have tried to get more information from Marcel about Pierre's wife, don't you?'

Jacky nodded. 'And have you?'

'No, he wouldn't tell me another thing.'

'No pillow talk?'

Debbie smiled. 'Oh, plenty of pillow talk…but not about Liliane.'

Jacky gave a sigh of relief. 'So that's the end of the matter.'

Debbie looked uncomfortable. 'Well, not exactly. There

was a little pillow talk when I told Marcel that you were having problems trying to compete with Pierre's so-called perfect wife. Marcel said Liliane was far from perfect—in fact, he thought that if you and Pierre were having problems it was about time that Pierre was told the truth about her. He said—'

She broke off as Marcel came into the room, carrying Thiery.

'Ah, there you are, darling… Hello, Jacky. Lovely to see you again.' Marcel bent to kiss her on both cheeks.

'Let me hold Thiery,' Jacky said, reaching for the baby.

She smiled as she looked down at the baby on her lap. Talking soothingly to him in French, she was rewarded with a wide, toothless smile.

'He's almost four months now, isn't he?' she said. 'I think I can see a couple of teeth outlined in the gums here.'

'We heard the teeth coming through last night, didn't we, darling?' Debbie said wryly to her husband.

'We certainly did! Thiery was awake for hours and so were we. I'm glad I'm still on holiday and don't have to go into hospital until next week.'

He sank down on the sofa beside his wife and looked across at Jacky. 'Where's Pierre?'

'He'll be along soon,' Jacky said quickly. 'I came to see if I could give Debbie a hand but it's all under control apparently.'

'You can go up and play with Thiery and Emma for a while if you like,' Marcel said. 'Emma likes to play with Thiery on his play mat each evening. But at seven years old she sometimes becomes a bit too boisterous with him. It's good for Thiery to kick his legs on the floor so we like her to encourage him to be active, but one of us has to be there to supervise.'

'I'd love to,' Jacky said, holding the baby carefully as she stood up.

As she carried Thiery upstairs she told herself that it was better she didn't confront Marcel before supper. But if she felt the conversation at the supper table was heading towards anything dangerous, she would have to speak out.

'Jacky, I didn't know you were here!' Emma came rushing out of her bedroom and flung herself at Jacky. 'Now we can speak English. I hardly ever speak English…except with my mummy.'

Jacky held Thiery tightly in her arms as she bent down to kiss Emma.

'I've just finished my homework,' Emma said importantly. 'I had to draw a picture of my family. Baby Thiery, Mummy, Daddy… Marcel isn't my real daddy, you know. My first daddy was English. But he got fed up and left Mummy and me in London. That was where Mummy was a doctor in a hospital.'

The little girl paused for breath, but only briefly. Jacky had heard all about this from Debbie and wondered whether to stop Emma. But it was impossible to stop her in midflow.

'I was only two so I can't remember what he looked like—my real daddy, that is—except from the photo I used to put on my bedroom wall. I kept thinking he would come back but he didn't. When Mummy married Marcel I asked her if she thought my real daddy would ever come back. She said he might come back to see me but it was unlikely he would stay.'

Jacky hoisted baby Thiery over her shoulder. 'Shall we go into Thiery's room, Emma?'

'Yes, but I haven't finished telling you my story. There's lots more.'

'I'm listening, darling,' Jacky said as she sank down

on the window-seat that looked out over the garden. She would have felt she was intruding on private family secrets, except Debbie had already told her all this and more. She and Debbie had no secrets from each other.

Whenever they were together she felt as if Debbie was the sister she would have liked to have had. And Emma, with her worldly-wise, old-beyond-her-years air, would definitely have been her favourite niece! Somehow Emma reminded her of herself when she had been that age. Knowing most of what was going on around her but pretending to still be an innocent child. Just to please the grown-ups and their idea of what children should know!

Emma crouched at her feet. 'Well, anyway, when Mummy said she didn't think my real daddy was coming back to stay, now that she was married to Marcel and all that, I asked Marcel if he would take over as my real daddy and let me call him Papa. *Papa*—because we live in France, you see.'

Jacky nodded solemnly. 'And what did Marcel say?'

Jacky knew exactly what he'd said because Debbie had told her, but she wanted to hear what Emma made of the situation.

Emma smiled. 'He said he really liked the idea. He would be…oh, some big word…honoured? Would that be it?'

Jacky nodded. 'I'm sure that's what Marcel said.'

'Yes, Marcel said he would be honoured if I'd be his proper daughter. And he went over to London to where I'd been born and he saw somebody important in a big important building and…' Emma paused for a moment to catch her breath.

'And then, when Marcel and all these important people had written to my real daddy, Marcel came back and said he'd…he'd adopted me…? Is that the right word? I know the French word but…'

Jacky reached down with the arm that wasn't holding Thiery and hugged Emma. 'Yes, that's the right word.'

'I'll bring the drawing of my family down when we have supper. I'm staying up for the grown-ups' supper. Now I'm seven I often stay up late.'

'Would you like to show me where I can find Thiery's play mat?' Jacky said, anxious to get back on safe ground before Emma continued with the life story of her family.

'Oh, yes, it's in that chest.' Emma raced across the room.

The little girl carefully spread out the soft mat before sitting down at the edge to watch Jacky as she lowered Thiery onto it.

'Thiery loves kicking now!' Emma enthused. 'When he was first born I thought he was a bit boring…and I'd really wanted a sister to play with. I asked Mummy and Daddy to get me a sister next time. Anyway, Thiery is more fun now, I really love him. Come on, Thiery, kick your little legs in the air…'

Jacky smiled fondly as she watched Emma playing with her little stepbrother. She knew how hard it had been for Marcel and Debbie to overcome the obstacles that had threatened their relationship. But now they were so happy together. If only she and Pierre could…

'Jacky, I'm so glad you're Thiery's godmother,' Emma said. 'It means you're going to help Mummy and Daddy and me look after him all his life, doesn't it? So you'll always have to keep coming to see us, won't you?'

Jacky swallowed the lump in her throat. 'Yes, I will,' she said.

She had no idea how long she would remain in this part of France, but she would always make time to come and see her dear friends in this warm family. She'd become very close to all of them and it had made her so happy when Debbie had asked her to be godmother to her new baby.

Jacky could see that Thiery was tiring of the activity, his legs moving more slowly now. She bent down to pick him up and cradle him in her arms.

Debbie came in and smiled. 'Thanks ever so much, Jacky. And thank you, too, Emma. Whatever I would do without my big daughter to help me, I don't know! Are you going to go and change for supper, darling?'

'Sure you can manage without me, Mummy?'

'I've got Jacky to help me,' Debbie said solemnly as she reached over to take Thiery into her arms.

Jacky continued to speak English after Emma had gone. She took a deep breath as she faced her friend. 'We have to talk, Debbie. You know how I feel about disillusioning Pierre. I love him so much and I couldn't bear to see him hurt. Please, will you make sure that Marcel doesn't—?'

'Jacky, Marcel is a law unto himself. He will only do what he thinks is right for Pierre…and for you.'

'I know Marcel thinks it would be right to set the record straight but—'

'I think it would be right for both of you. When Pierre knows the truth about Liliane, you can step in and—'

'Debbie, I've explained to you before. It's not just a case of toppling the icon! Pierre is very family-orientated. If he realises Liliane wasn't as perfect as he thought she was and decides he's free to marry again, I'm not the right woman for him. Pierre will need a wife who's prepared to give him children—'

'There's Pierre now,' Debbie interrupted, as she heard the doorbell ringing. 'I'm going to feed Thiery now. Marcel is preparing drinks. Go down and meet Pierre.'

Jacky sighed. 'He's no idea what he's in for tonight!'

Debbie sat down in the low antique feeding chair that Jacky had given her when Thiery was born. It was such a perfect present. Jacky had told her she'd found it in the *marché aux puces* in Paris. Jacky was such a good friend. She was very fond of her and she couldn't bear to see her so miserable.

She looked up. 'I love this chair you bought me. It's so comfortable, ideal for baby feeding.' She began unbuttoning her blouse.

Jacky was still standing by the door, as if unwilling to go down to greet Pierre. 'Debbie, you will—'

'Jacky, I promise I won't let Marcel spoil our supper. Anyway, Emma will be with us so he won't speak out in front of her. Maybe afterwards Marcel will have a little chat with Pierre…'

Jacky hurried away down the staircase. She didn't want to think about it. She'd done all she could to stop the secret coming out.

Marcel and Pierre were standing in the hall. Jacky wanted to make sure she didn't give them any time alone together before supper. If Marcel was planning to drop his bombshell, it would be easier to cope with when everyone had enjoyed a good supper. If Marcel drank a few glasses of wine he might even forget…

'Hello, Jacky,' Pierre said.

As he watched her coming down the stairs he was thinking how beautiful she looked tonight. Well, she always looked beautiful to him. Her cheeks were flushed, as if she'd been hurrying. He loved the way the skirt of her floaty dress wafted around her. She didn't often wear a dress but when she did she looked stunning. So feminine, so adorable, so desirable…

He was waiting at the bottom of the stairs. He took her

hands and drew her towards him. He could see her glancing across to see if Marcel was watching. She was probably worried about displaying too much affection in front of Marcel. But Marcel was a close friend and he must have realised how much he cared for Jacky.

He bent his head to kiss her. As his lips touched hers, she remained stiff, unlike her usual pliant self. Something must be worrying her. He'd make sure they had time to themselves later so that he could hold her in his arms and help her relax.

'Pierre, Pierre!' Emma came running down the stairs, her arms outstretched for a hug. 'Where's Christophe?'

'He was very tired from his first day back at school. Nadine is going to put him to bed early.'

Emma nodded understandingly. 'And he's only five, isn't he? I'm seven so I'm coming to the supper party tonight.'

'Come and have a drink, everybody,' Marcel said, leading the way into the sitting room.

Jacky felt relieved that Emma had joined them. As Debbie had pointed out, at least Marcel would keep quiet a bit longer.

'The supper was perfect, Françoise,' Jacky said, as she helped Debbie to carry the plates into the kitchen. 'The cassoulet had such a succulent flavour. I love the old traditional French dishes. Reminds me of my childhood in Normandy.'

Françoise beamed with pleasure. 'That was my grandmother's recipe. I'm glad you enjoyed it. Emma helped with the pastry for the fruit flan, of course.'

'The pastry was home-made?'

'Of course! I make everything myself.'

'Françoise is a complete treasure,' Debbie said, as she

spooned coffee grounds into the cafetière. 'You must relax now, Françoise. Are you coming to have coffee with us out on the terrace?'

'I can't drink coffee in the evenings,' Françoise said. 'Keeps me awake. I'll take a mug of hot chocolate up to my room and watch television. There's a programme I'm looking forward to. Would you like some hot chocolate, Emma?'

Emma, thrilled at being allowed to stay up for grown-up supper, said she would love some chocolate and could she watch television with Françoise? Debbie said it would be better if she drank the chocolate in her own room and went to sleep as soon as possible. It was school again in the morning.

'I'll take you upstairs, Emma,' Jacky said.

She wanted to escape the adults for a while. There had been a certain brooding atmosphere around the table that evening. Emma had livened things up as she always did. But it had been like the calm before the storm. Jacky was sure that once Emma was out of the way, Marcel would drop his bombshell.

He meant well, she knew. He was the most caring man and would think this was all for the good, but she didn't want to be there to see Pierre's face when he learned the unthinkable truth about his perfect wife.

'Come on, Jacky!' Emma grabbed her hand. 'Let's go up now! I won't have any hot chocolate, Françoise, thank you. Will you read me a story, Jacky?'

'Why don't you read a story to me? Your reading was very good the last time I heard you.'

Emma smiled happily. 'OK. Come and choose what you'd like to hear. I've got some new books I read in the holidays.'

'I'll make fresh coffee when you come down,' Debbie

said, coming out into the hall as Jacky and Emma began to climb the stairs. 'Don't keep Jacky up there too long, Emma.'

'I won't.' Emma raced ahead.

'I'm happy to spend time with Emma,' Jacky said, looking down at her friend through the banisters at the bend in the stairs.

'I know you are…but Pierre may need you.'

Jacky groaned inwardly. 'I'll be down as soon as I can.'

It was like being on a roller-coaster that wouldn't stop and kept on moving towards inevitable disaster.

She went into the bathroom to supervise Emma brushing her teeth then taking a shower, followed by brushing her damp hair, finding a clean pair of pyjamas and taking her time putting them on. The little girl chattered incessantly during the whole procedure of getting ready for bed, but Jacky enjoyed the fact that she couldn't possibly worry when she was being entertained all the time.

At least, she thought she wasn't worrying, but she realised that above the noise of the chatter she was trying to listen for the sound of the voices downstairs. They'd gone out onto the terrace now so she couldn't hear a thing.

'That was a lovely story, Emma,' she said as she took the book and closed it. 'Your reading is excellent.'

'I like reading,' Emma said, yawning sleepily as she held up her arms towards Jacky. 'Goodnight, Jacky.'

'Goodnight, Emma. Sleep well.'

Jacky went back into the bathroom to clear up the mess. Better get downstairs now. She looked in the mirror, running a hand through her hair. She looked a bit dishevelled but nobody would notice.

Now for it!

CHAPTER TEN

As soon as Jacky got downstairs she knew the bombshell had been dropped. There was an ominous silence everywhere. She could almost feel the atmosphere as she walked out onto the terrace.

Marcel and Debbie were sitting alone. Neither of them was speaking. They looked up warily as Jacky arrived.

'Where's Pierre?' she asked anxiously.

'He's somewhere out in the garden,' Debbie said.

Jacky walked to the edge of the terrace and looked out. By the glow of the lights arranged at the edge of the path she could see him. He was standing absolutely still. Should she go out and interrupt his thoughts? Probably better to leave him by himself for a while. Let him come to terms with what had just been revealed.

Marcel stood up. 'Let me get you some coffee, Jacky.'

'Thank you.'

She turned round and went to sit down next to Debbie.

'How did it go?' she asked Debbie quietly.

'I'm not sure. Pierre said very little. But I think it affected him badly.'

'What did Marcel say? What did he tell Pierre about Liliane?'

Debbie hesitated. 'He told him everything he knew about an affair she had when they lived in Australia...and I found it hard to listen to. No, please, don't ask me the details, Jacky. Pierre will explain as much as he wants you to know. I...I think he's really going to need you now.'

Jacky looked up as she heard Pierre's footsteps crossing the terrace.

'Jacky, I think we should leave now,' he said quietly. 'Thank you for supper, Debbie.'

'Marcel is making some more coffee,' Debbie said quickly. 'Won't you stay a little while longer, Pierre?'

'I really think we should go,' Jacky said quickly, as she stood up.

She kissed Debbie goodbye and walked over to Pierre.

He took hold of her hand as he led her over to the terrace door.

'I've made the coffee,' Marcel said, meeting them in the doorway. 'Look, why don't you sit down again, Pierre, and we can all discuss what—?'

'Thank you for your concern, Marcel,' Pierre said evenly. 'But I need some time to think about what you've just told me. One day I'll be able to thank you for enlightening me, but at the moment…I'm in shock.' He hesitated. 'It wasn't entirely unexpected, as you probably gathered. I had my suspicions. But I didn't know the extent to which Liliane had gone to deceive me.'

He broke off, his voice choking.

Jacky squeezed his hand. 'Let's go home, Pierre,' she whispered.

It was only when she got into the car that she realised she had no idea which home they were going to go to.

She looked across at Pierre as, grim-faced, he drove towards the gates.

'Will you come back to my apartment for some coffee?'

He took his eyes from the road and turned to look at her for an instant. By the light of a streetlamp she saw the haunted expression on his face.

'You'll be wondering what all this is about. I ought to tell you what's happened.'

'Only if you want to,' she said.

'I do,' he replied, as he slowed to take the roundabout at the bottom of the hill.

As they began to drive along the sea front, Jacky looked out across the water, shimmering in the moonlight.

'Would it help if we walked along the beach?' she asked.

He glanced out to sea for a moment. 'Yes, I think it would. It looks so calm and peaceful out there.'

He steered into a parking bay and switched off the engine. He took her hand as they walked down the sandy path leading to the beach. They walked for a while in silence, Pierre deep in thought, Jacky waiting for him to say something.

They were walking towards the sea, the top of the waves glinting with the cold light of the moon. On any other occasion Jacky would have found it very romantic. But tonight she was simply worried about Pierre.

There were some rocks near the sea. Jacky steered their path towards them. As they sat down, Pierre began to speak about what had happened, as she'd hoped he would.

'As you've probably gathered, Marcel told me things about Liliane which he thought I should know.' He picked up a pebble and hurled it towards the sea, as if trying to release some of the tension he was feeling. 'I was angry at first but now I'm glad he told me.'

He turned to look at her and in the moonlight she saw the haunted look had disappeared. He looked strong again, more like the Pierre she knew. She waited quietly for him to continue.

'I remember that Liliane had been depressed for a while. She gave up her job at the hospital in Sydney because she said she felt tired all the time, too tired to go out to work. She begged me to take her back to Paris, said she was homesick and tired of Australia. I agreed we would go back to Paris. I had a good career record and was confident I could get a good position in a French hospital.'

He took a deep breath. 'But the depression and ill health continued in Paris.'

'And you had no idea why she was depressed?'

'I didn't know what had triggered it,' he said, a hint of harshness creeping into his voice. 'Marcel enlightened me tonight. He told me that after we'd gone back to Paris, a medical colleague had confided in him that he'd had an affair with Liliane.'

'Had you suspected anything?'

'Not at the time it must have happened,' he said. 'But I had my suspicions…afterwards. Marcel told me that Liliane had become pregnant by this so-called friend of ours…'

'Oh, no! How awful!'

He lowered his voice to a mere whisper. 'Apparently, she'd undergone a secret abortion at a small clinic in a rural area miles from our hospital, to avoid any of our medical colleagues hearing about it. All the dates that Marcel gave me tie in with the times that Liliane took holidays and days off by herself.'

'How could she have been so sure it wasn't your child?' Jacky asked.

He hesitated. 'We'd stopped having any kind of marital relationship. We were sleeping in separate rooms. I'd almost got to the point where I was going to suggest we split…but then—it must have been after she'd had her abortion—she became very depressed and completely dependent on me. I couldn't leave her.'

'But I thought you were so happy together!'

He drew in his breath. 'We were...until she had this affair. Marcel told me her lover finished with her soon after the termination.'

Jacky picked up a handful of sand, allowing the grains to sift through her fingers over the rock she was sitting on. The sand felt cold and damp. Summer was coming to an end. Some of the deep sadness that Pierre must be experiencing seemed to creep into her bones.

'So, do you think the fact her lover had finished with her triggered Liliane's depression?'

'I don't know. Probably. She saw a psychiatrist when we got back to Paris who said she wasn't clinically depressed. He could find nothing wrong with her physically or mentally. He seemed to think she had too much time on her hands. During one session he asked her if she'd ever thought of starting a family.'

Jacky leaned forward, listening more intently.

Pierre sighed as he shifted his position and leaned back against the cold rock. 'I vividly remember the day Liliane came home and asked me what I thought about the idea of starting a family. She said she didn't feel very maternal and wasn't sure if she would make a good mother.'

'So you hadn't suggested the idea of starting a family, Pierre?' Jacky said evenly.

He shook his head. 'No, but once we'd started to discuss it I thought it would be an excellent idea and I told her so. I said it was what I'd always wanted.'

'So it wasn't you who persuaded her against her will?' she persisted.

'No, it wasn't but...but I always felt that if I'd vetoed the idea she wouldn't have gone ahead. She was completely ambivalent about it. I've always been convinced

that my enthusiasm swung the balance in favour of starting a family.'

She turned and gripped the sides of his arms. 'But
you're not to blame, Pierre! You shouldn't feel guilty that
your wife died in childbirth.'

He took a deep breath. 'It's awful but I don't feel guilty
any more...not after what Marcel told me tonight. I
feel...horrified because—'

He broke off, clasping and unclasping his hands, staring
ahead at the sea. 'It's so awful when I think about it.
Marcel told me that the clinic where Liliane's abortion
was performed was closed down soon afterwards. Some
of the staff were unqualified and inexperienced. After
Liliane died in Paris, when I studied the post-mortem report I was mystified by the fact that it said her death was
caused by the fact that her uterus had been damaged in a
previous pregnancy or termination. This had caused it to
rupture when she went into labour.'

'And did you query it?'

'Of course! The pathologist repeated that his findings
were correct, so I concluded that Liliane must have had
a termination before we met. It saddened me, but I thought
it had happened before our marriage so I tried to put it
out of my mind...until Marcel told me tonight about the
termination at a dubious clinic. He said that when he'd
heard about Liliane's death in childbirth he'd wondered
if he should confide his suspicions to me. But at the time
he hadn't thought it would serve any purpose.'

'You've been left in the dark for far too long. How do
you feel now?' she asked gently.

'I'm not feeling anything at the moment,' he said in a
barely audible voice. 'Thank you for listening, Jacky. Just
having you here...' His voice trailed away.

He took a deep breath. 'I'll take you home now.'

They walked slowly back up the beach to the car. Outside her apartment he opened the passenger door and took both her hands in his. 'I won't come in for coffee. I...I'm not very good company for you tonight. It's been such a shock. I need to be alone for a while.'

'I understand.'

He bent to kiss her lightly on the lips. She savoured his kiss but it was all too brief. She felt as if she'd lost him already. He took her key and opened the door for her, standing back so that she could go in. She still hoped he might change his mind. But he was already turning away, heading back to the car.

She went up the stairs with a heavy heart. She would see Pierre tomorrow. He needed time to grieve for the wife he hadn't really known. The wife who'd deceived him and broken his heart and had paid for it so dearly.

In the days that followed Marcel's revelations, Pierre appeared to function perfectly at the hospital. In fact, when she watched him, Jacky could see that he was at his most professionally efficient in everything he did. Nobody watching him would have realised the emotional turmoil that must have been going on inside him.

She'd decided she would avoid seeing him in off-duty situations unless he specifically asked her out. But he didn't. He was polite but distant with her, seemingly withdrawn whenever they had a few minutes together at the hospital when they weren't actually working. She longed to reach out and touch him, to tell him he could confide in her, but she didn't.

Ten days after Marcel's revelations, Pierre had to go to a five-day medical conference in Paris. He didn't phone her, she didn't phone him. There was simply a big gap in her

life that she didn't know how to fill. Work was the anti-
dote to her loneliness...and her worry that their brief affair had ended.

Her one hope was that the change of environment
would renew and refresh his spirits. Turn him back into
the man she loved.

Sitting at the desk in her office, as she tapped in the date
on her final computer report of the day she was reminded
that the conference in Paris was due to end the next day.
Pierre would be back in St Martin for the weekend. She
wondered if she would see him and if she did, how would
he be? Would he have resolved his problems?

There was a knock on the door. *'Entrez!'*

Without looking up, she continued to stare at the screen
as she listed her last patient's injuries. Football injury,
meniscectomy advised by orthopaedic...

'Still at work. You should have been gone ages ago.'

'Pierre!'

She looked up at him, relieved to see a captivating
smile on his handsome face, once more. Her heart began
to thump madly.

'I didn't expect you back until the weekend.'

'The main conference finished at lunchtime. The rest
was just socialising, exchanges of ideas, that sort of thing.
I had more important matters to think about so I drove
straight back here.'

He drew her to her feet, putting his hands under her
arms, lifting her off the ground and twirling her around.

'Pierre, have you been drinking?'

He laughed as he set her down on the floor again. 'Not
a drop. I told you, I just drove back from Paris. But I feel
intoxicated with happiness. I'm sorry I didn't phone. It's

taken me a while to come to terms with all the deception that went on in my marriage.'

His expression became serious again. 'While I was in Paris, I spent a little time visiting the arrondissement where Liliane and I lived. I pressed the bell of the apartment where we used to live. A young man's voice on the entryphone told me to come up. A young couple were living there. I simply told them I used to live there. They offered me a drink. I thanked them but declined, saying I had to move on. I'd simply wanted to revisit my past again....'

'You must have been...deeply affected by your surroundings.'

'I glanced around the living room but it was all changed. I felt strangely calm again. Calmer and happier than I've felt for a long time. As I went back down the stairs, I knew that I'd finally said farewell. The worries of the past that had haunted me for so long had finally disappeared.'

He breathed a deep sigh of relief. 'It's ancient history. I'm completely free! I want to move on now. I want us to be together. Let's—'

He broke off, his eyes aglow with happiness as he looked down at her. She'd never seen him look so completely at ease with himself.

'Jacky, come out with me tonight and help me celebrate my new freedom. Just imagine...no more guilt! No more worrying about what happened in the past! Just you and me. We need to talk, to make decisions. I want it to be the most memorable evening of our lives...so far...'

'Pierre, it's wonderful to see you so happy,' she said, feeling thankful that the Pierre she loved had returned to her.

He held her closer, his lips coming down on hers. She

gave an inward sigh as their lips blended. She closed her eyes and gave herself up to him as his kiss deepened. But as she pulled away, the rational part of her mind began to nag. She no longer had to compete with the perfect wife, but if Pierre suggested they move on to a more permanent relationship, she knew she couldn't comply. She would have to come clean.

'I've already spoken to Christophe and Nadine on the phone,' Pierre continued, his voice conveying pure joy. 'They've both given me permission to go out this evening, so I'll reserve a table somewhere special. We'll take a taxi so I don't have to drive. We'll drink champagne to celebrate and...'

He paused and looked down at her. 'You're very subdued, Jacky. Are you feeling all right?'

His enthusiasm was infectious but she still felt apprehensive. It sounded as if he was planning something exceptionally memorable for tonight and she couldn't help thinking it might be the one situation she would find impossible to handle. He'd only just recovered from one shock. How could she turn him down if he was planning to ask what she thought he was? But for his sake she would have to try.

But she couldn't explain her reasons for keeping their relationship temporary if they were dining in a busy restaurant. People all around them, possibly listening in.

'I'm a little tired, that's all. It's been a busy day.' She hesitated. 'I don't really feel like going out tonight. Why don't you come to my apartment and I'll make supper? Say in about an hour?'

'If that's what you really want... OK, I'll bring some champagne. We can celebrate at your place.'

*　*　*

She barely had time to pick up a quiche and some salad from the shops, have a quick shower, get dressed and reheat the vegetable soup from the fridge before Pierre arrived.

He was still in an ebullient mood. She accepted a glass of champagne as she stirred the soup.

As they clinked their glasses together she couldn't bear to think that she might have to quash his hopes if he should suggest a permanent relationship.

He reached forward and switched off the hob. 'Come and sit down. I'm too excited to eat anything for a while. I just want to talk to you.'

She was holding her champagne precariously in one hand as he removed the spoon from the other, leading her away from the kitchen into the small sitting room. His arm was round her waist as he drew her down with him on to the sofa. Slowly he kissed her and she shivered with sensual longing. It seemed such a long time since they'd been together, really together...

She smiled as she came up for air. 'I've spilt some of my champagne.'

'Let me get you a refill.'

He went out to the kitchen, returning with the bottle to top up her glass. 'I hope this will be a night we'll remember all our lives. Jacky, there's something important I want to ask you...'

She put her glass down on the small table at the side of the sofa. Her heart was beating wildly as she waited.

'I'm going to do this in the time-honoured way,' Pierre said in English as he sank down on one knee. 'Jacky...Jacky, will you marry me?'

'Oh, Pierre...' She paused, desperate to try to soften the blow. 'I can't. I really can't. It wouldn't be fair to you.'

He sat down next to her, his arms around her, holding

her as tears began to flow down her cheeks. 'Why wouldn't it be fair? What do you mean?'

'After all you've been through, you deserve to have a wife who can give you children, brothers and sisters for Christophe. A woman who can be a proper wife to you.'

'I don't understand. You're the only woman in the world for me. I'll never want anyone else. Why?'

'I could never go through pregnancy and childbirth again. I lost my baby. The consultant told me I would need major surgery to have the remotest chance of conceiving again. And even in the unlikely event that I become pregnant, the delivery would be dangerous and traumatic.'

'Darling, my precious darling, I only want you. I wouldn't put you through childbirth again. We have enough children in our lives. Having Christophe with us will be as good as having ten children. And you're godmother to Thiery and very close to Emma. Why would we want any more children?'

He took a tissue from the sidetable and stroked away the tears from her cheeks. 'We have everything we could ever want, my precious. I want you to be my wife…for richer for poorer, as they say in the English wedding ceremony, in sickness and in health…to love and to cherish…till death us do part…'

'Don't, Pierre. You'll make me cry again,' she said, realising that her tears were now tears of happiness. 'Don't you think you would regret the fact that your wife couldn't give you a proper family?'

'We are a proper family already! You, me, Christophe… I don't want to have to share you with any more family members!' He gave her a wry grin. 'But we can get a cat and a dog, if you think we should fill the house a bit more… A budgerigar, a parrot, a few dozen goldfish…'

'Oh, Pierre, you're so wonderful!' She hesitated. 'I love you so much. I only want what's best for you.'

'*Chérie*, you are the best thing that ever happened to me,' Pierre said, completely serious again. 'And I only want what's best for you. I'm sorry your experience of childbirth was so traumatic. I feel deeply for the hurt that you suffered when you lost your baby. You've come to terms with the fact that you won't be able to have children. That's not what you want, but you've accepted it. Don't you think it would be better to go through life with me, sharing Christophe with me, happy in our own family unit together? Christophe already loves you as if you were his own mother and I love you so much that I can't contemplate life without you.'

She studied the completely sincere expression on his handsome face and her rational and emotional feelings seemed to fuse in agreement.

'You've finally convinced me,' she said quietly. 'I feel as if a great weight has suddenly been lifted from my shoulders. I've been carrying this problem around with me for so long.'

Pierre sank down to his knees again. 'Let's go back to the beginning, shall we? Pretend my first proposal was merely a rehearsal.' He cleared his throat. 'Jacky, will you marry me?'

'Yes…yes, I will, I will, I will,' she cried joyously.

He stood up and scooped her into his arms. 'Shall we break with tradition now and have a rehearsal for the honeymoon?'

She smiled up at him. 'I think that's a wonderful idea…'

* * *

As Pierre had predicted, last night had been the most memorable night of their lives…so far. Jacky smiled as she thought of the many more to come.

But now there was a wedding to organise. She sat up and reached for the scribble pad at the side of her bed.

'What are you doing?' Pierre raised himself on one elbow and watched her fondly.

'I'm planning our wedding. You can help me.'

'First we need to set the date,' Pierre said. 'The sooner the better as far as I'm concerned. How soon could you move out of your apartment and into my house? I mean our house—that is, unless you prefer to choose another house, in which case…'

'I love your house…but not as much as I love you,' she said, as she put down the pad and leaned forward to kiss him.

She smiled. 'At least I won't have to find curtains for this bedroom now that I'm moving out.'

'Ever the practical one,' he said as he pulled her into his warm embrace.

'Oh, I can also be romantic,' she said lightly.

'Mmm…I had noticed…'

They were married at the end of October in the little church of St Martin sur mer. The church was packed with colleagues, friends and family as the bridal party arrived in the middle of a rainstorm. Marcel had said he would be honoured to give Jacky away at the wedding ceremony. Jacky clung to his arm as they hurried up the path. They were followed closely by the bridal attendants, Emma and Christophe.

They went through the porch into the vestibule of the church. Jacky could hear the organ music. The double doors were held back against the wall. Through the wide doorway, down the aisle, she could see Pierre waiting for her. This was her ultimate dream. The dream she'd thought would never come true.

'At least I didn't tread on my bridesmaid's dress this time,' Emma said, grinning happily as she shook out the damp folds of her pink satin gown. 'Do you remember, Jacky, how you had to put pins in my dress where the hem had broken down when I was Mummy's brides-maid?'

Jacky smiled. 'Of course I do. You make a very pretty bridesmaid.'

'And very experienced now,' Marcel said proudly, sur-veying his beautiful adopted daughter.

'I love your dress, Jacky,' Emma said, stroking the front of the skirt. 'Is it silk?'

'Yes, silk, with lace around the sleeves here.'

She looked down at Christophe. He was very pale and quiet, apparently overawed by the whole experience.

'Are you all right, Christophe?' she said anxiously, as she knelt down in front of the little boy who already felt like her own son.

Christophe pulled a wry face. 'This collar's a bit tight,' he said, poking a small finger inside the stiff white collar attached to the shirt of his page-boy outfit.

'Let me loosen it,' Jacky said, undoing the clasp at the back. It flopped around a bit now but that was preferable to her darling Christophe being in discomfort.

'They're waiting for us, Jacky,' Marcel reminded her quietly.

'Just give me a few seconds more,' Jacky insisted, as she made sure that Christophe was happy.

The little boy put his small arms round her neck. 'I'm so glad you're my mummy now.'

'And I'm so glad you're my little boy,' she whispered.

She took hold of Marcel's arm, stepping forward down the aisle, her heart full of joy as she drew nearer and nearer to the wonderful man who would soon be her husband...

EPILOGUE

'CAN I hold her now?' Debbie said, as Jacky finished changing two-week-old Suzanne's nappy.

Jacky smiled. 'If I can hold baby Marguerite.'

Debbie smiled back. 'Let's swap over, shall we?'

Three-week-old Marguerite closed her eyes as she lay quietly in Jacky's arms. Jacky looked out through the bedroom windows, across the garden towards the sea.

'A bit windy today,' she remarked.

'Are we talking about our babies or the weather?'

Jacky laughed. 'Both. Do you realize, it's our first anniversary next week? Pierre wants to celebrate quietly but I'm going to talk him into a party. I want to have all our friends from hospital here, and all the obstetrics team who saw me through and gave me my miracle baby.'

'You made the miracle baby, you and Pierre,' Debbie said, looking down at Suzanne, who was sleeping peacefully in her arms. 'I'm so glad you went ahead with your pregnancy, even though some of the obstetrics team hadn't advised it.'

'It was such a shock when I found out I was pregnant! I couldn't believe it. Actually, as soon as we were married, I asked Pierre not to use a condom. I mean, because of my medical case history I never expected to get pregnant. It was totally unplanned. I was thrilled when it was confirmed that a baby was on the way.'

'I remember when you told me. You were over the moon! But at the same time, I could tell you were apprehensive about whether you would be able to carry your baby to term…and how difficult the birth would be. I didn't say anything but…'

'I was scared stiff, to be honest! But I knew it would be worth taking the risk. Pierre was apprehensive right the way through. He treated me like Dresden china…still does. That's why he's against the idea of an anniversary party. I expect I'll agree with him. We can have a party later.'

'What a beautiful view!' Marcel walked in and surveyed Debbie and Jacky sitting by the French windows that led out onto a balcony. 'And I'm not talking about the garden or the sea. Two lovely mothers with their daughters, discussing the idea of a party to celebrate…'

'You were listening in, weren't you?'

'Your voices carried down the stairs, Jacky,' Pierre said, walking across to put his hands on his wife's shoulders. 'If you really think you're strong enough for a party, I'll agree with you.'

She smiled. 'Let's discuss it later.'

Debbie stood up. 'I've got to be going now.'

'I'll put my daughter in her cot,' Pierre said, tenderly reaching down to take his wonderful baby Suzanne in his arms. He held her closely against him, revelling in the way his precious daughter clung to him.

Debbie said goodbye and carried Marguerite away.

Pierre drew up his chair near Jacky's. 'So, what have you girls been discussing while I was away?'

'We were saying what a difference a year makes! Who would have thought I would be a mother?'

'Darling, you were so brave. I was so worried about you.'

She stroked his cheek, looking up into his eyes. 'I know you were. But you were so supportive. Sometimes too supportive! All those tests and examinations you made me go through!'

'I wanted to make sure that the pregnancy wasn't going to be too dangerous. That's why, when your obstetrician advised you spend the last two months in hospital, I insisted you take his advice.'

'I didn't want to go into hospital. I didn't want to sleep in there without you. But I'm glad I did. When the labour started…'

'It was very traumatic for you, wasn't it?'

'Yes, but it was quick! I expected a precipitous birth but that was…' She broke off, searching for words to describe what she'd experienced.

'I believe you said it had been excruciating when I arrived on the scene,' Pierre said quietly.

'Did I? I don't remember. I was heavily sedated by then.'

'One thing's for sure, the emergency team couldn't have been on the scene quickly enough if you'd been at home. There could have been serious problems for you and Suzanne if…'

His voice trailed away. He couldn't bear to think about what might have happened to his precious wife and daughter.

He stood up and gently drew her to her feet so that he could enfold her in his arms.

'Since we married you've made me happier than I ever thought possible,' he whispered huskily. 'I love you, Jacky.'

'And I love you.'

She swallowed the lump in her throat. Every day of her marriage had been special. Even through her difficult pregnancy and labour, she'd been so happy that Pierre was going to be with her for the rest of her life.

The sound of voices brought her out of her reverie. 'That sounds as if Nadine has arrived back with Christophe.'

'Maman, Maman! I've drawn you a picture of my little sister.'

Christophe was already hurtling up the stairs like a mini-tornado.

He rushed through the bedroom door, a big smile on his face. 'Papa! *Tu es déjà retourné de l'hôpital!* What do you think of my picture? Do you think it looks like Suzanne?'

'Absolument! Regarde, chérie!' Pierre handed the picture to Jacky.

She held it at the side of Suzanne's cot. 'A true likeness. We'll have it framed. Suzanne's first portrait.'

'Drawn by an artist, as yet unknown,' Pierre said solemnly.

Christophe grinned happily. 'Can we go to the beach now?'

'It's a bit chilly for Maman, but I'll take you there for a little while,' Pierre said.

'I'll put a warm coat on and come with you,' Jacky said quickly. 'Nadine will look after Suzanne. She'll sleep until we get back.'

Pierre turned to look at her. 'Are you sure you feel strong enough?'

'I'm fully recovered! Soon I'll be as good as new.'

She smiled up at him, feeling a sensual shiver running through her as she saw the tender, romantic expression in his eyes. Their romance was still very much alive…and always would be…

0805/03a

MILLS & BOON®

Live the emotion

THE DOCTOR'S SECRET SON
by Laura MacDonald

When Luke left the country, he left Ellie's life. The
distance between them made it easier for her
not to tell him she was pregnant with his child. It
also made it easier to cope with her heartbreak.
Suddenly, he's back – and working at her practice!

A NURSE' S SEARCH AND RESCUE
by Alison Roberts

Tori Preston loves her new career in Urban Search
and Rescue – and she's enjoying the company of her
mentor, Matt Buchanan. But Matt is raising four
nieces and nephews alone – and Tori's not looking
for any new responsibilities...

THE FOREVER ASSIGNMENT *by Jennifer Taylor*
(Worlds Together)

Now that Kasey Harris is part of the team, the
Worlds Together aid unit is ready for its assignment.
But head of the team is gorgeous surgeon Adam
Chandler – and he and Kasey have met before...

Don't miss out!
On sale 2nd September 2005

Available at most branches of WHSmith, Tesco, ASDA,
Borders, Eason, Sainsbury's and most bookshops

Visit www.millsandboon.co.uk

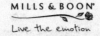

FREE

4 BOOKS AND A SURPRISE GIFT!

We would like to take this opportunity to thank you for reading this Mills & Boon® book by offering you the chance to take FOUR more specially selected titles from the Medical Romance™ series absolutely FREE! We're also making this offer to introduce you to the benefits of the Reader Service™—

- ★ **FREE home delivery**
- ★ **FREE gifts and competitions**
- ★ **FREE monthly Newsletter**
- ★ **Books available before they're in the shops**
- ★ **Exclusive Reader Service offers**

Accepting these FREE books and gift places you under no obligation to buy; you may cancel at any time, even after receiving your free shipment. Simply complete your details below and return the entire page to the address below. You don't even need a stamp!

YES! Please send me 4 free Medical Romance books and a surprise gift. I understand that unless you hear from me, I will receive 6 superb new titles every month for just £2.75 each, postage and packing free. I am under no obligation to purchase any books and may cancel my subscription at any time. The free books and gift will be mine to keep in any case.

M5ZEE

Ms/Mrs/Miss/Mr...Initials ....
BLOCK CAPITALS PLEASE

Surname ....

Address ....

....

....Postcode ....

Send this whole page to:
The Reader Service, FREEPOST CN81, Croydon, CR9 3WZ

Offer valid in UK only and is not available to current Reader Service™ subscribers to this series. Overseas and Eire please write for details. We reserve the right to refuse an application and applicants must be aged 18 years or over. Only one application per household. Terms and prices subject to change without notice. Offer expires 30th November 2005. As a result of this application, you may receive offers from Harlequin Mills & Boon and other carefully selected companies. If you would prefer not to share in this opportunity please write to The Data Manager at PO Box 676, Richmond, TW9 1WU.

Mills & Boon® is a registered trademark owned by Harlequin Mills & Boon Limited.
Medical Romance™ is being used as a trademark. The Reader Service™ is being used as a trademark.